Memoirs of a Monster Hunter

Memoirs of a Monster Hunter

Nick Redfern

New Page Books
A Division of The Career Press, Inc.
Franklin Lakes, NJ

Memoirs of a Monster Hunter
Edited and Typeset by Gina Talucci
Cover design by Lucia Rossman/Digi Dog Design NYC
Printed in the U.S.A. by Book-mart Press

To order this title, please call toll-free 1-800-CAREER-1 (NJ and Canada: 201-848-0310) to order using VISA or MasterCard, or for further information on books from Career Press.

The Career Press, Inc., 3 Tice Road, PO Box 687,
Franklin Lakes, NJ 07417
www.careerpress.com
www.newpagebooks.com

Library of Congress Cataloging-in-Publication Data

Redfern, Nicholas, 1964-
Memoirs of a monster hunter : a five-year journey in search of the unknown / by Nick Redfern
p. cm.
ISBN-13: 978-1-56414-976-3
ISBN-10: 1-56414-976-5
1. Monsters. I. Title.

GR825.R43 2007
001.944--dc22

2007016717

Dedication

For Danny, Melissa, and Sue.

Acknowledgments

I would like to offer my sincere thanks to the following people:

Phil Groff, Bobby John Craig, Chester Moore, Ernie Sanders, Jeannie Tatum, Ken Cherry and the Dallas-Fort Worth Mutual UFO Network, Kris Scott, Ryan Wood, Lisa Farwell, Sandy Grace, Monica Polania, Fredy Polania, Dan Salter, Craig Woolheater and the Texas Bigfoot Research Center, David Vassar, Kevin O'Brien, Paul Devereux, S. Miles Lewis, Jim Marrs, Dr. Robert M. Wood, Lisa Shiel, Gloria Smith, Alex Montana, Stephen Adair, Brad Crump, Danny and Melissa Adair, Sue Adair, Scott Herriott, Matthew Williams, Jim Moseley, Jim Castle, Scott Willman, Greg Bishop, Mac Tonnies, and Bill Konkolesky.

Special thanks must go to Ken and Lori Gerhard; Paul Kimball, Jim Kimball, Findlay Muir, John Rosborough, and everyone at Red Star Films; Phyllis Galde and all of the staff at *Fate* magazine; Rob Riggs; Jonathan Downes, Richard Freeman, and everyone at the Center for Fortean Zoology; Linda Godfrey, for the interview; authors Marie Jones and Joshua Warren, for providing the back-cover blurbs for this book; Sandra Martin; Patrick Huyghe; my literary agent, Lisa Hagan, for all of her outstanding work; everyone at New Page Books, particularly Michael Pye, Kirsten Dalley, and Gina Talucci; and my wife, Dana, for her love and support.

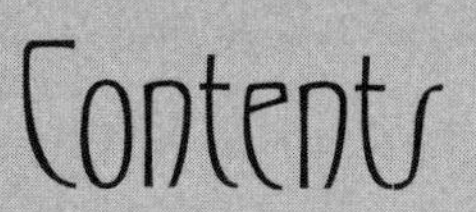

Contents

Introduction

It was 1 a.m. on a pitch-black, cold, English morning in early March 2001 when the loud electronic buzz of the alarm clock woke the man from a dead sleep. Bleary-eyed, he leaned across, muted the offending racket, and then headed for the bathroom, where a warm shower and a shave awaited him. He dressed in his usual attire: a black t-shirt, black jeans, and black biker jacket. After a quick breakfast of hot, milky tea and thickly buttered toast, he headed for the front door with a large suitcase and a small bag in tow. As he stepped outside and scanned the starry sky, an icy blast of wind caught him square in the face. But the man was unperturbed: He was on a mission.

Barely 48 hours later, he was due to speak at a weeklong UFO conference on the other side of the world; a coach from the nearby city of Birmingham that was due to take him to London's Heathrow Airport eagerly awaited. The man loaded his suitcase and bag into the trunk of the car, turned on the ignition and the radio, and drove the seven miles to the coach station. Not a soul was on the winding moonlit roads; indeed, the only sign of life was the occasional fox that darted nervously into the darkened hedgerows when it was caught in the headlights of his typically compact English vehicle. The coach trip to Heathrow was uneventful, and the man managed to grab a few hours of sleep, curled up on two adjoining seats, before the long-haul flight from hell ultimately lead him to the blistering climes of the Nevada desert.

Meanwhile, deep in the heart of west Texas, another journey was about to commence. Two women—one, a middle-aged divorcee, and the other her daughter, a striking 6-foot-tall blonde with a liking for incredibly short, leopard-skin mini skirts and black, spike-heeled stripper boots—were also destined for the Nevada conference. The daughter was not particularly interested in UFOs: Psychic phenomena and ghosts were more her cup of tea. She was in between jobs, and was staying, for a short while, at the home that her mother and grandmother shared, which was in a small and isolated town called Littlefield, situated among sprawling fields of cotton, and not much else, approximately 40 miles west of Lubbock.

And when, several weeks previously, the mother had asked her daughter if she wanted to accompany her on a road trip to a seven-day conference on UFOs, the daughter thought for a moment and replied: "What else am I going to do here all day? Watch tumbleweeds float by?" That was a yes. The pair loaded the mother's gas-guzzling Cadillac with all of the essentials that would be required for their adventure, and headed off onto the highway.

As they drove away, the girl waved out of the passenger-side window to her pet shar-pei dog, Charity, who was sitting at attention on the doorstep, and who would be taken good care of by the girl's grandmother for the next week. The wrinkly hound stared intently at her momma for a few moments, and then happily waddled off to the comfort of the back yard, where she contentedly lay under a shady tree and ate ants for the rest of the day.

Meanwhile, back at Heathrow Airport, the black-garbed Englishman sat around, aimlessly thumbing through the pages of a celebrity gossip magazine, while taking swigs from a large bottle of chocolate milk, a product to which, by his own admission, he was practically addicted. A smile came to his face, however, when he noticed four familiar figures approaching him that he had met previously at various UFO conferences in the United Kingdom: Ian, Simon, Neil, and Steve, devotees of everything flying and saucer-shaped. Needless to say, they did what most English friends do at any airport at 6 a.m. when there's nothing else to do: They headed for the bar. Several hours later and suitably relaxed from the effects of the always-powerful British beer, the friends were airborne and bound for the United States.

The long and drawn-out journey was, thankfully, a blur for the five guys. Having landed at Las Vegas's McCarran International Airport and successfully negotiated Customs, where the man, perhaps unwisely, told the less-than-impressed and stern-faced Customs agent that his purpose for coming to the United States was to present a lecture on government conspiracies and UFOs, the five commandeered a shuttle bus and settled back into their seats for the 90-minute journey to their final destination: the Flamingo Hotel and Casino, deep in the heart of the city of Laughlin, Nevada.

The trip to Laughlin was a surreal one: With the sun having set on the stark desert and its craggy, mountainous surroundings, it looked as though they were embarking on a journey across the barren surface of the Moon. In fact, an hour or so into the trip, one member of the group quipped: "This must be where NASA faked the moon landings." They all nodded and laughed, unsure if this was intended as mere jest or something more.

By the time they arrived at Laughlin, which can best be described as Las Vegas's little brother, the group was beginning to feel the full effects of jet lag. After checking into the Flamingo and briefly taking a look at the casino, they all reluctantly retired to their respective beds at what was an embarrassingly early hour for a Saturday evening. The man made a mental note never to tell his friends back in England that he was in bed by 9 p.m. on a weekend night. He knew that they would not forgive him for committing such a heinous crime.

On the way to his room, the man bumped into Christine Birdsall, the wife of *UFO Magazine* editor Graham Birdsall, who was also lecturing at the event. They hugged, chatted for a brief moment, and promised to meet up the following day for lunch. Although the Englishman did not know it, the Texan chick and her mother had also just arrived. Not wiped out by jetlag, however, they decided to hit the casino for a raucous evening of gambling and frozen margaritas.

Early on the following morning, the man from across the Atlantic woke refreshed and ready for some fun. He headed down to the floor where the conference was due to take place and ran into the organizers, Bob and Teri Brown. This was not his first time at the Flamingo; he had spoken there at the Brown's 1998 event, too. Greetings were exchanged with Bob and Teri, and with his trusty box of slides handed over to the audio-visual guys who were preparing for his 11 a.m. lecture the following morning, the man was now free of commitments for the rest of the day and night, and headed off to grab a sandwich and a cold drink.

On the way to the restaurant, he spied a friend from England, Tracie, and her fiancé Jim Peters. Tracie had organized several UFO conferences in England during the course of the last few years. Jim, along with Jose Escamilla, was one of the foremost experts on the mystery of the Rods: strange, flying creatures that were being seen across the world with increasing, and alarming, frequency, curiously invisible to the naked eye. Cameras were the only means to capture the elusive beasts that looked, and sounded, similar to something out of the pages of a nightmarish H.P. Lovecraft novel.

Jim and Tracie met at a 1999 UFO conference that was held in the north of England, which was organized by a group known as LAPIS: the Lancashire Aerial Phenomena Investigation Society. The LAPIS events were always wildly entertaining, with flowing booze and outrageous behavior the norm. The pair kept in touch through the next few months, visited each other's countries, cemented a relationship, and, now, Tracie was planning to move to the States permanently to be with Jim in California. Although the man from England did not know it at the time, only 24 hours later he and the girl from Texas would embark on the first steps of a journey that ultimately led them down an identical path to that of Tracie and Jim.

My name is Nick Redfern. I am that man from England, and this is the story of my five years of chasing monsters, mysteries, and the macabre in the United States of America.

1

The Story Begins

At around 8.30 a.m., two days after arriving in sunny Laughlin, I entered the elevator that would take me down stairs to the floor where I was due to lecture in approximately two hours. Having done so, I strolled into the adjacent restaurant and grabbed a bowl of cornflakes and a glass of orange juice. I had been to the United States previously, but had never quite realized until now how much of an overriding love affair Americans have with food. Truly gargantuan figures dressed in baggy XXXL t-shirts, shorts, and baseballs caps, who were too fat to walk or even waddle, rode merrily around the restaurant in little, motorized carts, filling their already-overflowing plates with mountains of bacon, sausage, and eggs, while simultaneously gulping down gallons of diabetes-inducing soda. And then they went back for seconds.

I watched this gastronomic, artery-blocking atrocity with hypnotic fascination for about 20 minutes, and then made my way to the conference room and took a seat near the back. I vaguely recognized a few faces in the audience from my previous time at Laughlin in 1998, but there was no one around who I could truly say with certainty that I knew. None of the English guys were there yet. So, I had one last look at my lecture notes, then settled back to watch the first talk, which was probably the most hilariously entertaining one of the week, delivered in fine style by crop circle researcher Andy Thomas, a man who, I have no hesitation in saying, could easily have carved for himself a career as a stand-up comic.

As I continued to scan the room, I noticed two women walk through the doors and head in my direction. I did not know it at the time, but it was the mother and daughter from Texas. "I wouldn't mind a bit of *that* for the week," I said to nobody but me as the daughter approached.

"Is anyone sitting here?" she asked.

"No, you're fine to sit there," I replied with a smile, checking out the rest of her buxom form.

"Thanks," she purred quietly, in a fashion that almost had me salivating.

I heard her mumble something like, "That guy has a speaker's badge on," and I could see the pair watching me and glancing sideways. At that moment, all three of us burst out laughing when a strange looking fellow walked into the conference room with an aluminum pyramid-shaped device perched precariously upon his balding head.

"Why does he have that on?" asked the girl, her eyes widening in amazement and shocked awe as the odd figure shuffled toward us.

"Maybe he's expecting bad weather," I offered. Again, we all laughed and I caught the girl's eye for several seconds. *Well, the day was getting off to a pretty good start*, I thought. Then it was time for Andy to present his lecture, and silence descended upon the audience. Damn, I thought, what a time for the conversation to be curtailed. And on top of that, before Andy's lecture was over, I was required to go behind the stage to get ready for my own talk. When I finally got off the podium after my 90-minute lecture, I quickly headed to the back of the room, but the pair was gone. Completely vanished. I cursed silently. Still, there was nothing I could do about it, and I headed off to a small room adjacent to the conference area, where I was due to be interviewed for a cable TV show on UFOs. As I reached the room, I saw the girl about 20 feet away; she was heading back to the auditorium.

"Hi, I enjoyed your talk," she said, still purring like a kitty in heat. I was just about to reply when a voice shouted: "Nick, we need you—now!" It was Ted Loman, the one-eyed, patch-wearing producer of the aforementioned UFO show. The gods of fate were definitely working against me today, I thought. I looked at the girl, shrugged my shoulders, and headed off with Ted. I glanced back and caught her smile once again, before she vanished into the darkened depths of the lecture room. I might be able to salvage things, after all. But as events transpired, I didn't have to. Around 4 p.m., researcher and author Lloyd Pye came up to me and said: "Nick, there's a girl in the audience asking to meet you."

"Is she American? A tall blonde?" I asked.

"Yeah, that's her," Lloyd replied.

Cool, I thought. I must have done something right, after all. There was a 15-minute break between lectures, and I followed Lloyd through the milling crowd and spied the girl and the older woman, still near the back of the room. "Nick, this is Dana. Dana, this is Nick," said Lloyd, matter-of-factly, and then promptly walked off!

But the good thing about Lloyd's brief introduction was that it allowed the two of us to break the ice ourselves. It was, of course, all small talk to begin with. I learned that the woman with the girl named Dana was her mother, Alex, and that they would be here for the whole week. The whole week: I said a silent "Hooray!" I had a prearranged meeting later that evening with Ryan Wood, a researcher overwhelmingly obsessed with the Roswell "crashed UFO" controversy, who I had met in England back in 2000, and Graham Birdsall of *UFO Magazine*, and so I asked Dana: "Why don't we meet in the restaurant around 9 p.m.?" She said yes and the world was already a happier place.

At precisely nine, I entered the restaurant, and there she was waiting patiently. She had already eaten with her mother, but I was famished and chomped down a chicken sandwich. We split an ice-cream sundae and then headed for the bar and drinks. As we sat and chatted, it transpired that, although from other ends of the world, we had shared a lot of common ground. We were exactly the same age, we both had an interest in various aspects of the paranormal, and both of us were big fans of loud music. While my tastes ran—

and still run—to punk rock and not much else, Dana was a lover of classic American rock. We sat for hours chatting, getting to know each other, discussing our respective lives and cultures, our respective hopes and dreams, and had a damned fine time.

Around midnight, we were done with the drinks and I asked Dana if she would like to take a walk. I was, of course, delighted when she said yes. It was a starlit night, and the moon shone brightly as we exited the hotel and took a slow stroll down to the water's edge. Indeed, the atmosphere became one of almost magical proportions when a small rabbit crossed our path barely 3 feet in front of us and just sat there, staring at us, seemingly unconcerned by our presence. At the same moment, a large bird circling the hotel was caught in the glare of the powerful spotlight that was positioned on the rooftop of the hotel, and it took on a proud and magnificent golden glow. We smiled at each other, and continued to walk and talk. After a while, we reached a small bench, sat a while, and watched the river's water gently splash against the rocks, as what sounded like a million crickets chatted excitedly to each other. I had no idea of the nature of their conversations, but if they were similar to ours, they were doing just fine.

After 20 minutes or so, we headed back to the hotel and I asked Dana if I could do something. "What's that?" she asked. "This," I replied and I held her in my arms and kissed her gently—at first, at least. As the passion levels rose we headed upstairs. Yep, things were definitely looking good. Outside of her hotel room door, the Anglo-American lip-lock was renewed in fine fashion. But try as I might, I could not get Dana to come back to my hotel room for, ahem, "coffee." Nevertheless, it was a perfect end to a perfect night; we said our goodnights and retired to our respective beds. I'm sure I spent the whole night sleeping with a smile on my face.

The next day was a fine one: a small lunch and then an Italian dinner in one of the several restaurants that the Flamingo was home to. We wandered around the casino awhile, and I expressed my sheer amazement at the truly huge number of octogenarian ladies, all smoking like chimneys, and who, like preprogrammed robots, were pumping dollar bill after dollar bill into the flashing slot machines. What was most peculiar was the uncanny fact that these gambling grannies seemed never to sleep: the same ones were always there, regardless of the hour, always inserting their hard-earned dollars into the money-munching machines. The rest of the week was a good one, filled with romantic dinners and private moments in which two people who had met as strangers were now opening up their lives to each other.

It was after we had been at the conference for about three days that very strange rumors began to circulate. Indeed, they were rumors that sounded as though they emanated from the paranoid mind of a certified maniac. And perhaps they did. Whispered tales spread like wildfire among the attendees about people who had been "implanted in the backs of their necks" with alien-originated tracking devices. Moreover, those same implants allowed the aliens to control the person in question, to the extent that they could be "programmed" to become *Manchurian Candidate*-style assassins. Even worse: Something similar had supposedly occurred at the 2000 event 12 months previously, and several people who had returned this year were "not what they appeared to be." They had been "replaced" by "alien clones," again programmed to fulfill the intentions of some nefarious, extraterrestrial agenda.

It sounded akin to something out of the 1950s sci-fi movies *Invasion of the Body Snatchers* and *Invaders from Mars*. It was highly entertaining. It was complete bullshit. At least, I *thought* it was complete bullshit until I saw several people, all of whom *were* exhibiting genuinely odd marks on their necks, staring at me in a *very* strange way, not unlike a dog when it's just about to bite. I remember shaking my head in disbelief but still wondering: "Well, what if...?" Of course, I knew such things just couldn't be. Could they?

But that was not all: Countless people were complaining of dizzy spells, of pronounced vertigo, and feelings of nausea that seemed to plague them wherever, and whenever, they went. The rumor mill continued to churn, with the collective opinion of those affected being that they had been "microwaved" by the dreaded—and ubiquitous—"them." Ah, yes: "them." The veritable hallmark of the paranoid and the delusional. But most of those complaining about such maladies seemed quite rational. Again: It couldn't be, could it?

I never really knew what to think about it all. To be stuck in a Nevada hotel with alien-replacements and microwaved paranoiacs, amid a never-ending background of bleeps and squeals that emanated from a plethora of slot-machines 24 hours a day, was highly appropriate for an English author of all-things-paranormal, and whose whole life seemed to attract wackiness in a way that a pile of shit attracts flies. And believe me, among those who heartily disagree with my ufological beliefs, such a comparison has been made on more than one occasion. But back to the most important thing: Dana.

Some might say that this was merely a heady, holiday romance that thousands of people all around the world experience when they are away from home, and alcohol, partying, and physical attraction are all key factors. But this time, there was definitely that extra something there, too. We just seemed to gel. The romantic dinners, and the longs talks about anything and everything, continued into the early hours of the mornings, and our days were filled with laughter. But as is often the case in such situations, the time flew by, and we knew that the week was going to be over in the blink of an eye. In fact, it was. After the gala dinner on the Saturday night when time was definitely no longer on our side, we were both thinking: What happens now? It was a question that echoed around my brain for the entire night. Primarily because on the following day, I was due to fly back to England, and Dana and Alex were Texas-bound.

On the Sunday morning, we both did our packing in our respective rooms and met in the lobby. When I saw Dana, it was quite clear that she had been crying. We sat closely on the couch in the lobby and I said that I would e-mail her as soon as I got home, and that we would exchange phone numbers. "You promise?" she replied, with a look on her face that was a mixture of both delight and concern. I nodded with a smile and squeezed her hand. Dana would later admit, however, that even though she had a great time, and she hoped that this would not turn out to be just a week-long adventure, she secretly had a few doubts about whether I would really keep in touch, or if I would simply go back to England, never to be heard from again, and regale my mates with tales of the hot Texan chick I nailed.

Well, I *did* tell my friends back home that we had a fine time, but I did not want the week to be the end of things. And so, after the flight across the ocean, I powered up the computer and, distinctly bleary of eye, sent the first e-mail of what would ultimately turn out to be a lengthy exchange. It took Dana a few days to reply, however, as, on the journey back to Littlefield, Alex and her ended up getting caught in a severe snowstorm and had to stay in Sedona, Arizona for a while until the roads cleared. Day after day, and for hours at a time, we would be typing to each other, not to mention rapidly inflating the profits of the phone companies with lengthy, transatlantic calls.

A couple of weeks later, I was back in the States for a preplanned trip to the National Archives in Maryland (in search of government documents on strange phenomena that ultimately appeared in my 2003 book, *Strange Secrets*), and that afforded us more time to get to know each other. And it was then that I invited Dana to come and visit me in England for the whole month of May, close space which she eagerly agreed.

Driving Dana up and down the country and introducing her to my family and to close friends I have known since my school days, and,with whom I still hang out at every given opportunity, was a joy, and she got to experience for the first time an old English castle, the rolling, green hills of the north of England, 500-year-old haunted pubs, and a weekend in London that included Buckingham Palace, Big Ben, and the Houses of Parliament. She also met many of my good pals within the Fortean community, including Mark Birdsall, the editor of *Eye Spy* magazine, and my three closest friends within that same community: Jon Downes and Richard Freeman of the monster-hunting Center for Fortean Zoology, and crop-circle maker, Matthew Williams. Jon, Rich, Matt, and I were all booked to speak at the annual LAPIS UFO conference that month, and it was an ideal time for Dana to meet everyone in our usual, rowdy environments of off-the-wall lectures, free-flowing beer, and late nights of revelry. She loved it.

After a month of fun in Britain, it was time for Dana to head back to the States, and I began a six-week adventure traveling my homeland with Jon and Rich in search of all manner of unknown beast, an adventure that was chronicled within the pages of my 2004 book, *Three Men Seeking Monsters*. It was that six-week excursion that convinced me more than ever that the various mystery animals of this world such as Bigfoot, the Loch Ness Monster, the Mothman (and its British equivalent the Owlman), had supernatural origins rather than physical ones. Dana and I kept in touch, and within a week of completing our adventure, I was jetting back to the States again for a lengthy period—one that just about hit the limit on the amount of time I could spend in the States without securing a visa.

In the weeks that passed between Dana's return to Texas and my excursions with Jon and Rich that saw us rampaging wildly around England and Scotland in search of animals from the outer edge, Dana had moved from her mother's place in Littlefield to

Nederland, a pleasant southeast Texas town that was adjacent to Dana's hometown of Port Arthur, and which was situated on Texas's Gulf Coast. As a result, and as the hot summer of 2001 began in earnest, I flew from London to Houston International Airport, where Dana was waiting for me, and we drove the 90-minute moonlit journey to the house that she was renting from her dad, Danny.

The reason I came to America: my wife, Dana.

As I had learned from Dana, Danny was a powerful J.R. Ewing-type character in southeast Texas, who had carved out a highly successful career in the roofing industry, and who, along with his pregnant wife Melissa, and their son Danny, Jr., lived in a huge property in an area of Port Arthur called Pleasure Island. Dana's grandmother, Sue, lived in a spacious apartment that was affixed to Danny's house, and we would have a lot of good times cooking and eating out by the family's swimming pool as I got to know them all.

We stayed in Nederland for around a month; and in the same way Dana got to meet my friends, I got to meet several of hers, too (Biff and Sally will thank me for mentioning them), and I also experienced first-hand what it was like to grow up in a culture infinitely different to that of my own. Not only that, I had some amazing experiences during our time on the Gulf Coast, too. I saw wild alligators ambling leisurely across the winding roads of the nearby Louisiana swamps. I watched bobcats frolicking in the grasslands of the area. I tasted for the first time what looked like giant, radiation-mutated insects, but what I learned were actually crawfish. And I fell head over heels in love with the one meal that Dana cooks better than any other: gumbo. But after a month in Nederland, we were ready to undertake one of those things that I enjoy more than most: a road trip.

Even to this day I am amazed by the sheer size of Texas. Coming from Britain, where a person can travel the length of the country inside a full day, our journey from Nederland to Alex's home in Littlefield, which was our first destination, took something like eight hours—and we were *still* in the state of Texas. As Dana drove (I had not at that time secured an American driver's license, of course), I marveled at the scenery as we left Nederland. As a kid, I loved woods, rivers, and boggy marshes, and still do, and I stared endlessly at the view out of the passenger window. But as we headed toward what was known as the Panhandle, the scenery began to change, and the lush woods of southeast Texas were replaced by what seemed like hundreds of miles of utterly flat land, endless fields of cotton, and lots of places owned by someone called "Bubba," whose main activity seemed to be selling barbecued beef.

The sun was just beginning to fade when we finally arrived at Littlefield, and as we passed the old railroad tracks outside of town, I spied what I first thought was simply a big dog strolling along the tracks. As we closed in, however, and to my absolute astonishment, I became quite sure that what I was looking at was actually a large and powerful wolf. Not only that—whether it was a figment of my imagination I really don't know—but a sudden feeling of unreality overcame me, along with the sensation that the beast and I had a connection. Barely 100 feet away, the wolf's eyes locked with mine for a second or two, before it suddenly broke into a run and disappeared into the cornfields. I never saw it again; but I should have known that it was a sure signal of the weirdness that was to follow. Within a few minutes, we turned off the highway onto a small street and parked outside of a pleasant-looking bungalow.

Although I had spoken to Dana's granny, Gloria, on the phone on several occasions when I was calling Dana from England, this was to be the first occasion upon which I would meet her. Dana rang the bell, and a dark-haired lady with a small frame and a cheeky grin on her face came to the door, hugged Dana, and welcomed me into the delightful abode with open arms, as did Alex. I suddenly heard an ear-splitting yapping noise, and Alex's terrier, Chrissie, came running to see what all the fuss was about, as did a marauding, lumbering beast that charged headlong into the hallway, banged into countless items of furniture as it skidded wildly on the highly polished floor, and generally caused unrelenting chaos and havoc in the process. It was Dana's Shar-pei: Charity.

Charity was a big and muscular dog. She looked *very* imposing, and not at all like the sort of creature that you would want to get on the wrong side of. But it was all a sham. Charity was the gentlest, biggest baby you could possibly imagine, and she greeted Dana with unbridled love and excitement. After all, it had been a month since her momma had left Littlefield, and Charity had remained there, patiently awaiting Dana's return after four weeks with me in Nederland.

Dana hated to be parted from Charity, and I smiled broadly as the two excitedly played together in Alex's living room. Needless to say, Charity and I quickly became the best of friends. And after dinner, while noone was looking, most nights I would secretly spoil her with slices of bread, lunchmeat, and cheese, followed by lengthy walks around the town's park. On our return, she would invariably flop contentedly onto the carpet and happily snore and snort the rest of the evening away. It was a fine time, and Dana and I stayed at the house with Alex and Gloria for a month, just hanging out, and getting to know each other better.

When I arrived in the States, I e-mailed various monster-hunting research groups, UFO organizations, and paranormal societies with which I had previously been in touch, and informed them that I was going to be over for a while, and inquired if they would be interested in having me lecture for them. Three or four said yes, and they all got together to cover our expenses for various legs of the lengthy road trip that incorporated, among other locations, Roswell, New Mexico; Tucson and Sedona, Arizona; San Diego, Los Angeles, and San Francisco, California; Las Vegas, Nevada; the Hoover Dam; Lake Tahoe; Yosemite Park—and that ultimately ended in marriage.

2

Two Winged Things and a Wedding

Whenever I tell people that Dana and I got married on Halloween, 2001—and in Las Vegas, no less—I could always tell by the aghast looks on their faces that they were probably thinking that the ceremony was overseen by an overweight Elvis impersonator and at 2 a.m. in some cheap and tacky back room of a hotel. But nothing could have been further from the truth. The date was certainly appropriate for a couple that had a fascination with the paranormal, and the location was equally apt given our penchant for having a good time. But we ensured that our marriage day was a special one.

We booked a plush suite in Vegas's Flamingo hotel for six days (having flown there three days before the wedding), and flew Alex, Gloria, and Dana's brother, Stephen, in from Texas to attend, along with my mom and dad from their home in England. Also in attendance were various friends from Los Angeles, as well as a good friend of mine named Marcel who lived in Vegas, and who had what was possibly the most enviable job in the world. Marcel designed Websites for Vegas strippers and was paid handsomely for his skills—and in more ways than one, too. No wonder he was always smiling. Danny and Melissa, sadly, were unable to attend due to the fact that Melissa was—quite literally—about to give birth to their second child: Raygan.

The wedding day was an incredibly special one and I will never forget it. It was a warm, sunny afternoon, and the Flamingo's chapel where we tied the knot was set within the confines of beautiful, lush gardens. It was all that we hoped it would be. Dana looked stunning in her long, white dress and her cascading blonde locks that Stephen had carefully styled. My mom beamed throughout the event. Even though half a decade on, Alzheimer's has cruelly and forever robbed her of that day, at the time she could not have been more pleased for both of us. And neither could my dad, who continues to love Dana like the daughter he never had. Likewise, Dana's family had nothing but good wishes for us. After the ceremony, we headed for a splendid dinner and then back to our room for a night of romance as Mr. and Mrs. Redfern. It truly was a magical experience.

After our return from Vegas, the next step was for me to secure American residency. The process itself was not that taxing beyond the veritable mountain of paperwork that we had to complete. And so, after we filed that same paperwork, and as I waited for my Social Security card to arrive, we decided to get on with our lives. We rented a spacious house that we had stumbled upon in Littlefield that would be our home until March 2002, when we moved back to Texas's Gulf Coast. And now a little bit more about Littlefield....

The town itself was pleasant enough, and the people were extremely friendly and very hospitable. However, and I want to stress that this is certainly not a case of me speaking badly or critically, there was absolutely nothing to do there. Littlefield was situated in the Texas panhandle; and, as I have mentioned, it was surrounded by cotton fields, and cotton fields alone, that extended for miles. . .and miles. . .and miles in every direction. Indeed, aside from a Sonic, a gas station, and a couple of diners, the area was a literal Dead Zone. That is, unless you count the truly incredible number of gargantuan tumbleweeds that hurtled violently along the dusty streets of the town at every given opportunity. Amazed (Dana might say

My main memory of West Texas: the tumbleweed.

obsessed), by these things that I had only previously seen in Hollywood westerns of decades ago, I almost expected to see John Wayne moseying into town atop a white stallion.

And to my everlasting horror, Littlefield was situated within a "dry county"—a term that, coming from Britain where liquor, beer, and wine are integral parts of everyday life, I had no comprehension of. But when I found out that it meant "no alcohol for sale," and that, if in order to buy beer I was faced with a mind-boggling 70-mile round-trip to Lubbock and back, I was truly mortified and amazed. It was therefore inevitable that our time in Littlefield would be severely limited. However, for such a small town in the middle of nowhere, it certainly had a distinct air of high strangeness about it.

For example, the nearby city of Lubbock had been the location of a famous wave of UFO encounters in 1951 that collectively became known as "The Lubbock Lights." Similarly, only a short drive from Littlefield was the town of Levelland, from where, in 1957, there had surfaced a sensational series of flying saucer reports involving both local citizens and police officers, all of who had described close encounters on a lonely stretch of road late at night with a large, egg-shaped UFO. And Alex had heard tales of then-recent sightings of a semi-spectral "white Bigfoot," that had been seen crossing a road late at night, and only a stone's throw from where the UFO encounters of 1957 at Levelland had occurred.

I was not surprised, however. As my *Three Men Seeking Monsters* book had demonstrated, in locations where one strange phenomenon was present, there were usually several others, too.

And as that same book also demonstrated, I had come to the conclusion that Bigfoot, aliens, lake monsters, and a plethora of other diabolical "things" were all, in reality, nothing but ingeniously crafted smokescreens and projected imagery, behind which devilishly cunning and devious creatures operated in stealth within our environment. Reputedly known by the witches and wizards of old England millennia ago as "Cormons," they were emotion-sucking vampires from some unholy realm; Tulpa-like creatures whose existence in our world was inextricably, and somewhat precariously, linked to our willingness to believe in them. These shadowy entities generated imagery of bizarre monsters and beasts in an attempt to create high levels of stress and emotion in the person who saw them, and that could then be extracted from the witness in the form of psychic energy, thus providing the Cormons with their essential nectar-of-the-mind.

And if that were not strange enough, I learned that there was a rumor in town that an old bag lady who supposedly walked the streets of Littlefield by both day and night had, in the 1960s, worked alongside one of the most notorious characters in the history of the United States' Intelligence community: James Jesus Angleton. The scoop was that she had insider knowledge on the JFK assassination, which traumatized her so badly that she had forsaken her career and spiraled into a major depression, finally ending up living on the streets of the town. I never saw the woman, and neither did anybody else. And I never got to the bottom of the tale—and maybe a tale is all it was. But the strangest story of all was still to come.

When we moved to Littlefield, word soon got around the close-knit community that I had a "strange job." As one local put it: "He's like that Mulder guy off *The X-Files*—he investigates weird shit." True, but without the gun and badge that the FBI's most famous, albeit fictional, employee routinely utilized. However, in the same way that Fox Mulder had Dana Scully, I had my own Dana, too, something that had amused my mates in England to no end when they first learned of her name.

As a result, one day there was a knock at the door: It was an elderly couple, related to the guy who lived next door, and who had suggested to them that they speak with me. I invited them in and they explained that they had an unusual story that they were looking to tell, which concerned events that had occurred back in the mid-1940s when they were teenagers. According to the account, the first incident occurred in the early months of 1946 at an old, large house that, until the early 1960s, had existed on the edge of town, and where two aged and eccentric sisters lived in absolute seclusion.

Supposedly, on one occasion in the dead of night (when else?), a group of local kids scaring themselves stupid by walking around the old, dark building had seen two, 8-foot-tall, humanoid creatures climb stealthily out of the building's cellar.

Not only were the creatures 8-foot-tall, but they were also gray of skin, had large, leathery wings, and glowing red eyes. In other words, they weren't local folk. I think. The monstrous pair apparently turned sharply as they surfaced from their underground lair and stared intently at the kids, then broke into a hopping-style run, opened their immense wings, and soared majestically into the starlit sky. One interesting observation was that the limbs of the creatures looked almost hollow against the background of the full moon that loomed overhead.

Perhaps even weirder was the fact that as the kids exited the area at what was an unsurprisingly high speed, two of them caught sight of the elderly sisters, grinning maniacally at them out of a downstairs window of the house. The couple also informed me that a similar creature, if not one of the original two, was seen several months later by a terrified motorist standing in the middle of the local highway in the early hours of the morning while issuing a woeful moan. That, in essence, was the account. I had no idea if it was genuine; and, as the couple told me, the key witnesses in the tale had all gone to their graves at surprisingly young ages—all supposedly killed in a variety of seemingly unlikely accidents. I nodded, preferring not to air my deep suspicions that this was simply a tall-tale designed to determine how gullible I was.

Of course, all towns and villages—whether in America, Britain, Germany, Australia, Russia, or indeed *anywhere*—have their own, unique folktales and legends, and perhaps this was Littlefield's. Following on from this point, researchers Loren Coleman and Jerry Clarke told the story of the Momo—a tall, "smelly, red-eyed creature" that was haunting the woods around Louisiana, Missouri. Notably, one of the witnesses to the strange entity, Randy Emert, had said that in the woods there existed "an old abandoned house," around which "large footprints" had been found. Also, there was a "hole dug under the basement" of the old house, where, Emert thought, the creature had made its lair. The similarities between both cases did not necessarily mean that my informants had based their story on that of the Momo, but it was a possibility definitely worth keeping in mind, I thought.

But there was one thing that was genuinely intriguing about the Littlefield story that *did* strike a chord with me. As readers of my *Three Men Seeking Monsters* book will know, only months before this tale was told, a practically identical story had been related to me in the ancient British town of Glastonbury by a man named Colin Perks, who in 2000, after delving into legends concerning King Arthur, had received a hellish, midnight visitation from a creature that sounded astonishingly similar to the beasts of Littlefield.

The extraordinary fact that I was there, directly immersed in both tales, but quite literally on opposite sides of the world, only added to the unique bizarreness. My attempts to encourage the elderly couple from Littlefield to reveal the names of the primary witnesses failed. However, as a result of my experience with Colin Perks at Glastonbury only a short time before, I felt that this account, even though it remained unfortunately unresolved and somewhat open to interpretation, was one that went way beyond the mere realms of folklore and mythology.

We stayed in Littlefield until March 2002, when we decided to head back to Dana's home town of Port Arthur, which was roughly an hour-and-a-half drive from the city of Houston. As we rumbled out of town in a moving truck crammed with furniture, possessions, and Charity perched precariously between us in the cab, I had to concede that despite its remoteness, Littlefield was a seriously strange place indeed.

3

Tales From Taos

Not long after we moved back to Nederland, a man named Salvador, who lived near the town of Taos, New Mexico contacted me after reading an article I had written for Jon Downes' *Animals & Men* magazine on the subject of Bigfoot. To say that he had a remarkable tale to tell is an understatement, as will soon become graphically apparent.

And in a curiously coincidental situation, an elderly fellow named Dan Salter, whom I had very briefly met at the Laughlin UFO gig in March 2001, phoned me from Taos, too, and only four days after Salvador. Dan had initially approached me at Laughlin with a strange tale about how he was plugged into the U.S. government's secret UFO world, and confided that he had classified tales that he wanted to tell. As a result, and taking into consideration the fact that both Dan and Salvador lived relatively close to each other, Dana and I traveled there to meet both characters in mid-2002.

Taos was a place I liked a lot. It had a cool vibe to it, there seemed to be so much going on, and the architecture—some of which dated back to centuries ago was amazing. Indeed, it was around 6,000 years ago that nomadic hunter-gatherers passed through the Taos area, leaving behind arrowheads, potsherds, and pictographs; and in approximately A.D. 900 the first settlements began to appear throughout the Taos Valley, the ruins of which can still be seen to this day. In 1598, Don Juan de Oate arrived as the "official colonizer" of the Spanish province Nuevo Mexico, and a decade and a half later the area was teeming with Spanish settlers.

The so-called Pueblo Revolt of 1680 led to the killing of countless Spaniards who had made the area their home, and those who were not killed were driven from the area in droves. Thirteen years would pass before the area next saw a Spanish presence, when resettlement of the province began. During the course of the next century, chronic attacks by Plains Indians led to a distinct decline in the population of the area. However, when in 1866 gold was discovered in the local Moreno Valley, it inevitably led to an influx of new blood, and Taos began to boom.

Six years later, the Carson National Forest, which had been created from the Pecos Rover Forest Reserve, the Taos Forest Reserve, and parts of the Jemez Mountain Range, became an integral feature of the landscape. Coolest of all: Segments of the celebrated movie *Easy Rider* were filmed in and around Taos. It was a place I will always remember with fondness. Not to mention that for the entire time Dana and I were there it snowed furiously, only adding to the atmosphere.

Salvador was an intriguing guy, having inherited a considerable sum of money in his early 30s, he was retired by the age of 43, and now at age 48 lived, as he worded it, "on a permanent vacation" in northern New Mexico. As I sat in the living room of his spacious, Pueblo-style house, and dived into a fine lunch of chicken and rice, Salvador related to me a remarkable story of truly bizarre proportions. It all began, he explained, on an August evening in 1997. A keen astronomer, he had taken his truck out to a particularly remote spot north of Taos that was free of light pollution, and where he could set up his telescope and scan the night sky.

It was around 1 a.m., Salvador recalled, when he heard a strange sound in close proximity that "was like a high-pitched whistle, but that had a human feel to it. But, it was way too high frequency for a man." Salvador's curiosity turned to concern, and then to outright fear, he added, as the whistle was replaced by "an aggressive growl, and heavy footsteps, like something was warning me and marking its territory." Salvador estimated that the source of the ominous growling was within 30 feet of him. Disturbingly, he got the distinct impression that a hostile entity of some form was actively "circling" him and "getting ready to attack." That attack never came, however.

Salvador then painted an incredible picture: He sat tight in the back of his truck for about 10 minutes as the growling and heavy footsteps continued to torture his terrified mind, when suddenly, in the distance, he could hear the unmistakable sound of helicopter rotor-blades. The sound got louder and louder; however, he could see nothing in the dark skies—that is, until a large spotlight bathed the entire area, and the dark form of a black helicopter, adorned with a large white star on its right side, could be seen hovering at a perilously low level. Concerned by the unknown life-form apparently circling his truck, he stood up in the back of his truck and waved frantically in the direction of the helicopter.

Salvador told me: "I think that the pilot of the helicopter must have had night-vision, because as soon as I waved he headed in my direction." The pilot of the helicopter closed in on Salvador, who recalled that "dust was flying everywhere, and the noise was deafening." Suddenly, the helicopter rose into the air and its spotlight was focused upon an area no more than 50 feet from Salvador's truck. He could now see what had been causing all of the commotion: a 7-to-8-foot-tall, hair-covered creature that "looked just like what people say Bigfoot is." The beast, Salvador said, suddenly took off "at a real speed," with the helicopter in hot pursuit. Both disappeared from sight as the helicopter's light grew fainter and utter darkness returned. A shocked Salvador jumped into his truck and quickly headed for the safety of his home.

Salvador asked me, "What was the helicopter doing flying with its lights off in the skies of Northern New Mexico in the dead of night? What was the nature of the strange beast that had apparently set its sights upon him? And what on Earth was the connection between the two?" This was, without doubt, one of the strangest stories I had ever heard. Salvador and I speculated: Was there a clandestine military group that was trying to resolve the Bigfoot mystery by attempting to capture one of the elusive beasts? If so, had Salvador inadvertently stumbled upon their covert activities? I had to admit to Salvador that I had no answers; however, as Dana and I drove around the Taos landscape later that night, I kept a careful and watchful eye on both the skies and the landscape for both man-beast and helicopter. If either were out there in force on that night, they failed to put in an appearance for me. The mystery remained precisely that, but the mysteries of Taos were far from over.

Dan Salter was both a strange and an intriguing character, and he claimed to know the inside story of Roswell, crashed UFOs, dead aliens, and high-level conspiracies of truly dizzying varieties. Dan also claimed to be a recently retired employee of the ultra-secret National Reconnaissance Office. When I met Dan at a diner in downtown Taos on our second morning in town, I felt sorry for the guy; he was elderly and extremely frail, had recently suffered several strokes, which impaired both his physical health and his speech to a considerable degree, and here I was about to intensely grill him on UFOs for three hours.

Nevertheless, and thank goodness, Dan fully retained his mental faculties, and was highly motivated and upbeat. Over a wonderful Mexican meal and margaritas, he regaled me with entertaining tale after entertaining tale about his out-of-this-world exploits and his decades-long career as a Fox Mulder-like 007.

Yes, UFOs were real, Dan told me. Yes, an alien spacecraft had crashed at Roswell, and both it, and its extraterrestrial crew, were recovered by the American military. Yes, sinister aliens were abducting American citizens and implanting them with tracking devices for diabolical purposes that could only be guessed at. Yes, people had been killed by the government to hide the horrible truth. And yes, there were a number of "underground bases" in New Mexico where the aliens were undertaking all manner of horrific experiments on people for purposes so terrible that the government, powerless as it was to intervene, dared not reveal them to the oblivious masses. And Dan, as a direct result of his work with American intelligence, was privy to these, the most guarded of all UFO secrets.

Later at the motel, I carefully prepared a full summary report of the time spent with Dan. However, it was not so much the interview itself that fascinated me, but a series of photographs that I had taken that same day. After exiting the restaurant around 2 p.m., Dan and I climbed into his vehicle and headed to the home of one of his friends. I could not help but notice as I headed toward the vehicle that its license plate was very different from any other that I had ever seen.

Instead of being made up of a conventional combination of numbers and letters, it read: HQ INTERPLANETARY PHENOMENON SCIENTIFIC AND TECHNICAL COUNTERINTELLIGENCE WA 25, D.C. I took some photographs of this curious piece of evidence in the saga of Dan Salter, who would later assert to me that the license plate was a reference to a secret, military organization called the Interplanetary Phenomenon Unit, and was a retirement present from his friends and colleagues at the National Reconnaissance Office.

He said to me: "I know you saw my license plate on the car. I saw you looking at it. That was on the vehicle I had on base at the NRO, and it was given to me when I retired. I asked if I could show it to people and they said, 'Well, if we didn't want you to show it to people, you wouldn't have it.' So, I guess, that means I can show it to people. But those vehicles with the plates were never allowed off base."

As we concluded the interview, Salter had these parting words for me: "Nick, we've gotten to know each other over these last few days and I feel comfortable talking because I know you just want answers. There are other things I can tell you. I have to speak with a few people, but you might get some other old-timers speaking to you in the next few weeks." Evidently, the "okay" never came. And even though I repeatedly called the telephone number that Salter had provided me with, it always remained unanswered, and I never heard from Dan Salter again.

4

Fangs, Fur, and Files

In my book *Strange Secrets: Real Government Files on the Unknown*, I included a chapter on the unusual fact that a whole variety of government and military agencies in the United States and the United Kingdom had on record voluminous, official files pertaining to sightings of mysterious animals, such as sea serpents in the Atlantic Ocean; big-cats deep in the heart of the British countryside; and even what is arguably the world's most famous mysterious creature: the Loch Ness Monster.

For reasons that have always eluded me, and for as long as I can remember, I have had a fascination with strange animals, and particularly with werewolves. When the other little kids at school were reading the British equivalents of *Nancy Drew*- and *Hardy Boys*-style adventures, I was deeply engrossed in the study of all things lycanthropic, including learning how to summon up demonic werewolf-style entities from the Underworld, and even how to transform oneself into a salivating, hairy beast borne of a full moon. That never worked, however. In *Three Men Seeking Monsters*, I revealed the rich history of centuries-long sightings of werewolves in Britain, and detailed my own encounter with such a beast in August 2002, when, in the throes of "sleep paralysis," I received a visitation from some nightmarish, wolf-like creature that growled and snarled menacingly as it made its ominous way down the corridor to our bedroom. After a tumultuous struggle on my part to wake up, the beast vanished amidst an overpowering stench of brimstone. I decided to cut back on my daily quota of whisky after that. Well, for a while anyway.

And when I learned, in early 2003, that a respected journalist was researching a sighting in Wisconsin of a weird, werewolf-like entity that was apparently, and somewhat startlingly, the subject of an official file with the local authorities, I knew that this was a story I had to get my teeth into (or perhaps claws would be a better term, considering the circumstances). Armed with trusty tape-recorder, pen and pad, and a .357 Magnum loaded with silver-tipped bullets (okay, I confess, the latter *might* be a bit of artistic license), I set off on a quest to uncover the truth about the Wisconsin werewolf and the woman who was about to bring the beast's infamy to the American public, Linda S. Godfrey.

Born in Madison, Wisconsin, Godfrey, an author and journalist, was raised in Milton and currently resides with her husband in rural

Elkhorn. Godfrey is a professional cartoonist, teacher, and writer whose newspaper articles have garnered several awards, including a first place feature story from the National Newspaper Association in 1995 and 1998. But it was her book, *The Beast of Bray Road*, and her time as Wisconsin's very own unofficial werewolf hunter, that has put her at the forefront of one of the strangest stories of modern times.

"Linda," I began, "What is the background to the story of the Beast of Bray Road?"

She replied: "The story first came to my attention in about 1991 from a woman who had heard that there were rumors going around here in Elkhorn, and particularly in the high school, that people had been seeing something like a werewolf, a wolf-like creature, or a wolf-man. They didn't really know what it was. But some were saying it was a werewolf. And the werewolf tag has just got gotten used because I think that people really didn't know what else to call it. And these days you have so much Hollywood influence that it colors your thinking about your observations. So when anybody sees something that's an out-of-place animal, you get those images."

"And I guess it attracted your journalistic mind, too?" I wanted to know.

"Well, I started checking it out," Linda explained. "I talked about it with the editor at *The Week* newspaper here, and which I used to work for. He said, 'Why don't you check around a little bit and see what you hear?' This was about the end of December. And being a weekly newspaper that I worked for, we weren't really hard news; we were much more feature oriented. So, I asked a friend who had a daughter in high school and she said, 'Oh yeah, that's what everybody's talking about.' So, I started my investigations and got one name from the woman who told me about it. She was also a part-time bus driver."

"And what did she tell you?" I asked.

"In my first phone call to the bus-driver, she told me that she had called the County Animal Control Officer. So, of course, when you're a reporter, anytime you have a chance to find anything official that's where you go. I went out to see him and, sure enough, he had a folder in his file draw that he had actually marked *Werewolf*, in a tongue-in-cheek way."

I laughed. "That's kind of surreal."

Linda was careful to state: "Well, it wasn't, by any means, that he believed it was a werewolf; but people had been phoning in to him to say that they'd been seeing *something*. They didn't know what it was. But from their descriptions, that's what he had put. So, of course that made it a news story. When you have a public official, the County Animal Control Officer, who has a folder marked *Werewolf*, that's news." She added perceptively, "It was *very* unusual."

"That must have really kick-started you and the publicity surrounding the mystery." I offered.

"Yes," she told me. "It just took off from there and I kept finding more and more witnesses. At first they all wanted to stay private, and I remember talking about it with the editor and we thought we would run the story because it would be over in a couple of weeks. The story was picked up by *Associated Press*. Once it hit

AP, everything broke loose, and people were just going crazy. All the Milwaukee TV stations came out and did stories, dug until they found the witnesses, and got them to change their minds and go on camera, which some of them later regretted. And which I kind of regret—because it really made them reluctant, and kind of hampered the later investigation."

"Okay," I said, "so we have the background. But what, exactly, was it that people were reporting seeing?"

Linda's reply was more than intriguing. "They were all mostly saying that they had seen something which was much larger than normal, sometimes on two legs and sometimes on four, with a wolfish head. Some described it as a German Shepherd-like head, pointed ears, very long, coarse, shaggy, and wild-looking fur. One thing they all mentioned was that it would turn and look at them and gaze fearlessly or leer at them, and it was at that point that they all got really frightened. Everybody who has seen it—with the exception of one—has been extremely scared because it's so out of the ordinary. It was something they couldn't identify and didn't appear to be afraid of them. It would just casually turn around and disappear into the brush. It was never just out in the open where it didn't have some sort of hiding place. There was always a cornfield or some brush or some woods. So, that was pretty much the start of it."

"And it progressed from there big time?" I inquired of Linda.

She responded in the affirmative: "Yes. Once that got out, I started finding other people who called me and got in touch with me and I sort of became the unofficial clearinghouse. And we called it the *Beast of Bray Road* because I've always been reluctant to call it a werewolf. The original sightings were in an area known as Bray Road, which is outside of Elkhorn."

"What are the theories regarding what the beast might actually be?" I asked her, with mounting interest.

"Everybody seems to have an opinion about this that they are eager to make known and defend," Linda explained. "I personally don't think there are enough facts for anybody to come to a conclusion. I have a couple of dozen sightings, at least. A few of them are second-hand and they date back to 1936. And they aren't all around Bray Road. Quite a number of them are in the next county, Jefferson. I've had a woman write me who insists it's a wolf. And I think a lot of people subscribe to that theory; yes, it's definitely a wolf and can't be anything else. But that doesn't explain the large size. A lone wolf *can* travel by itself. And there *are* wolf packs in northwestern Wisconsin. Except this has been seen over so many years."

I continued the questions: "But that's not the only theory?"

"There's another possibility: I think a lot of these people are seeing different things. And that when they heard somebody else talk about something, there's a tendency to say, 'Oh, that must be what I saw.' There's really no way to know. And there are differences in some of the sightings. I've had people ask me, 'Are you sure this isn't Bigfoot?' Most of the sightings really don't sound like what people report as Bigfoot. But a couple of them do. There's one man who saw it in the 1960s in a different area of the county, who insists positively that he saw a Bigfoot, but he doesn't want anyone saying he saw a werewolf. And the terrain around here isn't really the typical sort of Bigfoot terrain of forests where people usually report these things. We do have woods and a big state forest; but it's a narrow band of forest. It's a lot of prairie and is not what you would think a Bigfoot would live in. But you never know. I've also had the baboon theory, which I find extremely unlikely."

"And I'm sure there are almost as many theories as witnesses," I commented.

"We've had all sorts of theories: mental patients escaping or some crazy guy running around. A hoaxer is another theory; that it's somebody running around in a werewolf suit. One or two could have been that but I tend to have my doubts about that [theory] because the incidents are very isolated and not close together. One of the sightings was on Halloween, but that's also one of the people who got a really good look at it and they're sure it wasn't a human in a costume. Otherwise, most of them have been really in remote locations where, if you were going to hoax, the person would have to have been sitting out there in the cold just waiting for somebody to come along. So if it is a hoaxer, my hat's off to them. But I tend not to think that's the case. I don't rule it out completely because once publicity gets out, things like that can happen."

"Are all the reports of a single creature or has it been seen in pairs or packs?" I asked Linda.

She thought upon her answer for a moment, then replied, "The only report—and it's a second-hand report—came from two hunters quite a bit farther north who saw what looked like two 'dog children' standing up in the woods. They were too scared to shoot when they saw them. They were not tall; they were juvenile looking, standing upright, which is what scared them. But otherwise it's a single creature."

Then I posed the inevitable question in a situation such as this: "Is there a tie-in with the werewolf legends about these creatures being seen when the moon is full?"

"Well, most of the sightings I receive aren't recent, and so people can't remember too well what the moon was like. But most of the sightings occur around the fall when the cornfields get big and there's really good hiding cover. So that's anywhere from late August through November. And I've had some sightings from the spring. But there are other theories as well for what is going on."

Linda continued: "Occasionally I'll get letters from people who say they are lycanthropes themselves and their theory is that this is an immature, real werewolf and it cannot control its transformation and that's why it allows itself to be seen occasionally. They are completely convinced of that. And there are people who believe it's a manifestation of satanic forces, that it's a part of a demonic thing. They point to various occult activities around here. There are also people who try to link it to UFOs. Then there's the theory that it's just a dog. One woman, a medium, thought that it was a natural animal but didn't know what it was. And there are a lot of people out here that do wolf-hybridizations, and I've thought to myself you'd get something like that. But that doesn't explain the upright posture. Then there's the theory that it's a creature known as the Windigo or Wendigo, which is featured in Indian legends and is supposedly a supernatural creature that lives on human flesh. But none of the descriptions from the Windigo legends describe a creature with canine features."

"And what, after all of your investigations, have you concluded lies behind the mystery of the beast of Bray Road?" I asked her.

"Well, part of the angle of the book is looking at this as a sociological phenomenon and how something that a number of people see turns into legend. And it has become that, a little bit. Personally, I'm still happy to leave it an open mystery; I don't have a feeling that it has to be pinned down."

"With the publication of *The Beast of Bray Road*, do you feel that you work is now over and—regardless of whether or not the mystery has been conclusively resolved—you can move on?"

Linda responded with a laugh in her voice: "I don't think people will let me move on. I thought I would have moved on eight years ago but people still continue to contact me and I try to help them as much as I can." As time progressed, in the wake of the publication of her book, Linda continued to receive countless reports of the beast. Indeed, in 2005 she produced a follow-up title: *Hunting the American Werewolf.* I was delighted when Linda asked me to write an introduction for the book, which, in my mind, is the finest study of North American lycanthropes. I stay in touch with Linda to this day and, sure enough, Wisconsin's very own werewolf hunter is still hard at work, still seeking the diabolical beast, whether physical, paranormal, or satanic, that stalks by both night and day the prairies of rural Wisconsin.

5

Monsters of the Big Thicket

On a sunny morning in early June of 2003, I was chatting by telephone with good friend and fellow monster hunter Jonathan Downes, and when he asked me what I was doing research-wise, I happened to mention that I was then deeply enmeshed in an investigation of the wild women of Texas. To which, in response, Jon exhibited positively uncontrolled enthusiasm and excitement. I explained to Jon that he should calm down, as I suspected that the image swirling around in his head was not quite the intended one, sadly. The wild women that I was talking about were very different. They were, and indeed still are, part of a rich Texan history encountering Bigfoot-like entities, feral people, and man-beasts. And by this time, having lived in Texas for two years, this was a subject with which I had become extremely well-versed.

Anyone even remotely interested in such legends, stories, and accounts will be acquainted with the large body of testimony pertaining to the Sasquatch of the great forests of Washington State, and the so-called Skunk Ape of the Florida Everglades. Less well-known, however, is the startling amount of very similar evidence that emanates from deep within the confines of the Lone Star State. Historically, the collective data is more than intriguing.

There was an incident involving a "wolf girl" that occurred during the early decades of the 19th century, at the Devil's River near Del Rio, in southwest Texas. So the tale went, the girl's mother did not survive her birth, and John Dent, the father, died during a thunderstorm as he was riding for help after his daughter was born. Concerned locals failed to locate the baby, and it was assumed she had been eaten by wolves. The story, however, did not end there. A boy living at San Felipe Springs in 1845 had seen several wolves and a creature with long hair covering its features, resembling that of a naked girl, in the process of attacking a herd of goats. Further, similar reports surfaced over the course of the following 12 months, and Apache Indians in the area asserted that they had found what appeared to be the footprints of a child among those of the local wolf population. Was this the child that many thought had fallen prey to a wolf pack?

A hunt was duly launched, and on the third day the girl was sighted and cornered in a canyon. The legend was seemingly true. She was not alone, however. Indeed, the girl was, quite literally, in the company of wolves, one of which was shot after it attacked the hunters. The girl was subsequently captured and taken to a nearby ranch, where she was locked in a room. But matters would escalate after sundown. As night fell, a large wolf pack that had heard the girl's eerie howling closed in on the ranch and surrounded it. Needless to say, the farm animals became terrified, and as a result of the mayhem that erupted, the girl was able to flee from the ranch, reuniting with her four-legged friends. For seven years, the girl disappeared into oblivion. However, in 1852 a surveying crew that was exploring a new route to El Paso caught sight of her on a sand bar on the Rio Grande—she was with two pups and quickly vanished, never to be seen again.

An equally intriguing tale commenced with an account of strange "barefoot tracks of two human beings" that had frequently been found in the settlements of Texas's lower Navidad in 1837. The tracks were relatively small, and were thought by the witnesses to have been made by both a male and a female. Guard dogs on local ranches and properties would, on occasion, react in a furious fashion when the mysterious visitors were believed to be prowling the area late at night and in the early hours of the morning. And there were even reports of the pair breaking into people's homes and stealing food.

According to the legend, a human skeleton was later discovered that led some to believe the wild woman's larger, male companion had died. What happened to the skeleton—if indeed it ever really existed—remains unknown. An initial attempt by a group of men in the area to hunt the wild woman down failed. On the second occasion, however....

It was a dark night, as it inevitably is in tales such as this, and a shadowy form loomed into view. Whatever it was, the unidentified visitor was slim and unclothed, but was curiously described as having a body covered in short, brown hair. The men tried to forcefully grab her, but once again she bounded out of the area with astonishing speed. The puzzle remained unresolved for years, until a group of men allegedly cornered a runaway male slave in the same area. This duly satisfied local newspaper editors, who concluded that the wild woman of the Navidad was nothing of the sort, and was, in reality, the aforementioned unfortunate slave who had escaped from his masters and had been living wild for who knows how long.

Given the fact that not everyone was convinced that the wild woman and the slave were one and the same, however, another attempt was initiated to try and resolve the mystery, once and for all. A team of hunters decided that a complete check of the nearby woods was necessary. After several fruitless searches, the team hit the jackpot when one of them reported seeing the wild woman running along an adjacent prairie. Men with lassos pursued the woman while others with dogs ensured that she could not make her escape into the dense woodland. Again, the woman outwitted the hunters, but at sundown that situation was to radically change.

Under a moonlit sky, the excitement of the previous several hours was beginning to subside when the hounds became agitated, which signaled the presence of, well, something. Not only that, the something was crashing through the bushes in the direction of the hunters. It was the wild woman. Again, she bounded across the prairie and attempted to head toward the thick forest. Whatever the wild woman was, however, she was no normal human being. The nearest hunter reported that his horse was so afraid of the woman that it refused to go near her. And the fact that she was, by this time, running as fast as the most agile deer didn't exactly help the situation, either.

By this time, the wild woman was coming perilously close to the forest and the lead hunter realized that it was quite literally a case of now or never. He spurred his horse on and threw his lasso. It missed its target and the woman made her escape into the dense and darkened forest. Although the attempted capture of the Navidad wild woman had ended in failure, one important point should be noted. The hunter had an excellent opportunity to note the appearance of the woman as they both charged across the prairie. Similar to others before him, the hunter described her as naked, with a body covered in short, brown hair, and wild eyes. It was further reported that the woman was allegedly carrying something in her hand, and later, a 5-foot-long, carefully fashioned club would be found in the area.

Was this, similar to the girl seen at the Devil's River, some form of feral person? Or did the account have more in common with America's most famous, or infamous, monster: Bigfoot? Or could the whole saga be relegated to the worlds of legend and modern-day mythology? The jury, perhaps inevitably, is still out. Moving on from tales of wild women from bygone years, I was intrigued to learn that, in the period between 2002 and 2003, modern-day Texas was quite literally full to the brim with very similar reports of man-beasts and Bigfoot-like entities.

One week before speaking with Jon Downes, I had met with Rob Riggs, the author of the book, *In the Big Thicket: On the Trail of the Wild Man*, which told the story of Rob's own, personal investigation of a whole range of cryptozoological mysteries in Texas, particularly Bigfoot and "Wild Men of the Woods"-style entities. However, Rob's book expanded into other, very welcome areas, and he weaved together an intriguing scenario that linked reports of Bigfoot-type creatures with a variety of other anomalous phenomena, such as UFOs, "Ghost Lights," alien big cats, and much more. *In the Big Thicket* offered notable and eye-opening conclusions regarding what Rob believed lay behind encounters of this nature.

Similar to me, Rob was firmly of the opinion that Bigfoot, and the many and varied cryptozoological mysteries that continue to both fascinate and flummox us, were paranormal in nature. Or at the very least, that the beasts possessed extraordinary mental powers that made it appear that way. A journalist and the former publisher of a series of award-winning community newspapers in Texas, Rob was a fascinating guy, and in May 2003 he took me out to the aforementioned Big Thicket: a huge, forested area in southeast Texas. Similar to many people not born and bred in Texas, I had always imagined the Lone Star State to be dominated by long stretches of desert and not much more. In some areas of the state, as I certainly knew from my time in Littlefield, that was true, but I was very surprised, and very pleased, to learn exactly how much of southeast Texas was dominated by lush forestland.

Welcome to the Big Thicket—the lair of the Deep South's Bigfoot

The Big Thicket truly lives up to its name: an 83,000-acre area of East Texas's Piney Woods, it is a sprawling mass of rivers, swampland, and incredibly dense forestland comprised of cypress trees, short-leaf pines, and huge trees of oak and beech, where, according to local legend, "You'll find every critter in there from crickets to elephants." Not quite true, but the Thicket *is* home to a whole host of beasts, including armadillos, alligators, panthers, bobcats, and an array of snakes. And had you been there 10,000 years ago, you would have been lucky enough, or *unlucky* enough (depending on your perspective), to run into bison, camels, tapirs, giant sloth, beavers, saber-toothed tigers, and ferocious packs of wolves. Three groups of Indians were historically associated with the early years of the Thicket: the Atakapas, the Caddos, and the Alabama-Coushattas. Interestingly, on several occasions, Rob had heard uncanny tales to the effect that some of the wild-men-of-the-woods style encounters that had occurred deep within the Big Thicket were not due to the presence of Bigfoot at all. Rather, so the stories went, they were the result of encounters with surviving relic pockets of those aforementioned tribes who were still secretly living within the heart of the Big Thicket.

Bragg Road—or Ghost Light Road, as it was known locally—was where most of the action occurred. It was situated right in the heart of the Big Thicket, and began at a bend on Farm-to-Market Road 787 that was just a short distance from Saratoga. In 1902, the Santa Fe Railroad had hacked a survey line from Bragg to Saratoga, bought right-of-way, and opened the Big Thicket forest with a railroad. Subsequently, the Saratoga train began daily trips to Beaumont, carrying people, cattle, oil, and logs. When the area's oil booms and virgin pine gave out, road crews pulled up the rails in 1934, the right-of-way was purchased by the county, and the tram road became a county road. And tales of the ghostly light started to gather steam in the 1940s, 50s, and 60s as more people traveled to the road.

Explanations for the Ghost Lights were varied and descriptive. Some people believed them to be merely the reflection of car headlamps; while, for the most part, the scientific community considered them to be gaseous substances. Other theorists suggested that the lights were similar to the so-called Marfa Lights (also of Texas), while there were also those theorists who mused upon the possibility that the Bragg Road lights were indicative of an ongoing UFO presence in the area.

Deep in the heart of the Big Thicket, Ghost Light Road has been the site of countless weird encounters with Sasquatch.

Even during daylight, I quickly deduced, the Big Thicket was an eerie location. And only minutes after pulling off the highway, Rob and I were onto Bragg Road and into the depths of vast areas of forest dominated by thick trees and foliage. And it was from here that numerous encounters with ape-men, wild men, ghost-lights akin to the more famous Marfa Lights, and spectral big cats with glowing eyes had been reported for decades. I spent several hours roaming deep within the woods, cutting a swathe through the trees, spying all manner of critter, and getting bitten by mosquitoes, while Rob pointed out to me where some of the more prominent encounters with man-beasts had taken place.

As evidence of the general weirdness that purveyed the area, consider the following from Rob, which was based upon an account provided by "John," the primary witness: "John's family home is on the edge of the Trinity River swamps near Dayton. One night he heard a disturbance on the porch where he kept a pen of rabbits. He investigated just in time to see a large, dark form make off with a rabbit in hand. John impulsively followed in hot pursuit, staying close enough to hear the rabbit squeal continuously, not really knowing what he was chasing or what he would do if he caught it. It was a short distance through thick woods to the bank of the river. Standing on the high bank in the moonlight, he watched dumb-struck, as what looked like a huge ape-like animal swam to the other side of the river, easily negotiating the strong current, and never letting go of the rabbit."

As Rob also stated, "Like its Bigfoot and Yeti counterparts, the Big Thicket wild man has reportedly left clear tracks on a number of occasions....An expert Big Thicket guide told me of several sets of unusually large barefoot prints he had once come across in the vicinity of Black Creek deep in the Rosier Unit of the Big Thicket Preserve and miles from the nearest paved road. He had thought they were a bit odd at the time, but just assumed that they had been made by an extraordinarily big, old boy. When I pointed out the problem with this assumption, he agreed that it was unlikely that any normal person, big or not, would be walking about barefoot in the Thicket, which has virtually every description of thorn, sticker, and spiny vine, not to mention stinging insects and snakes."

Similarly, and purely due to coincidence or synchronicity, three days before meeting Rob, I had interviewed an elderly man from the town of Nederland where Dana and I were living at the time, who had seen a large and lumbering ape-like creature crossing the road near the Big Thicket's Bragg Road late at night in the winter of 1978. The man described the beast as being around 7 feet in height, jet black in color, and with a head that sat squarely on its shoulders. The witness added that the creature moved slowly across the road, and swung its arms as it did so, but did not appear fazed or at all concerned by the fact that the headlights of the man's car illuminated its face. Interestingly, and in a situation that eerily parallels some of the more mysterious cryptozoological encounters on record, when the man came within around 50 yards of the creature, the engine and headlights on his car both failed. It was only when the creature had departed into the woods that the man was able to restart his vehicle again. As a result, he had become a firm believer in the theory that the Big Thicket wild man was some form of paranormal entity rather than a flesh-and-blood animal.

Yes, the Big Thicket was a very strange place. But I would not find out for myself exactly how strange for another two years.

6

A Menagerie of Monsters

Stories of lake monsters and sea serpents have long held a particular appeal and fascination for me; indeed ever since I first traveled to Loch Ness, Scotland with my parents as a 4-year-old. And so, I am always very pleased to be on the receiving end of intriguing reports from those claiming personal sightings of mysterious long-necked denizens of the deep. In the last week of October 2003, I had appeared on one of the more well-known U.S. radio talk shows dedicated to discussions of all things paranormal, conspiratorial, and mysterious, and I chatted for two hours with the host about my interest in the Loch Ness Monster and its assorted ilk.

As a direct result of appearing on the show, a number of people sought me out, including a former employee of the United States Air Force, who asserted that he had seen such a creature back in 1969 while vacationing in the vicinity of the Upper Klamath River. Beginning in the Cascades of Southern Oregon and extending down to Copco Lake, south of the California-Oregon border, the river is some 250 miles in length, and takes its name from the Native American term for "swiftness." However, the creature that Jeff Shaw and his wife claim to have seen on a summer's day nearly 40 years ago can hardly be termed swift.

According to Shaw, he and his wife had rented a pleasant wooden cabin on one particular stretch of the river. Most days, they would sit near the water's edge with a couple of bottles of white wine and a well-stocked picnic basket. As someone whose schedule with the military was incredibly hectic, said Shaw, the pair relished some much welcome peace and quiet while simultaneously communing with nature. And commune with nature they most certainly did.

The Shaw's had taken a 10-day vacation, and all was normal for the first half of the trip; however, it was six or seven days into their break from the rigid confines of the Air Force that matters took a very weird and dramatic turn. On the day in question, the Shaw's had driven 15 or 20 miles in search of a particular sandbank they had been told about that was apparently the perfect area for a private water-side feast. Unfortunately, they failed to locate the place in question, and so, as fate would have it, they stopped at a shady, grassy area some 200 to 300 yards from the edge of the water. And with blankets, wine, and a plentiful supply of food laid out, they enjoyed a romantic lunch under a warm and sunny sky.

It was perhaps a little more than two hours into their day of fun when Jeff Shaw's wife saw, out of the corner of her eye, what she first thought was a large black bear ambling along at the edge of the woods and heading in the direction of the water. Concerned, she whispered to her husband and pointed in the direction where the creature was maneuvering among the trees and the bushes. But a closer look revealed that it was certainly no black bear.

Jeff Shaw explained to me that as the trees and bushes became less dense, he and his wife were able to get a much clearer view of the animal that was "shuffling" toward the lake. At first glance, he said, the creature was continually obscured by the woods, and therefore initially appeared to be only about 6 or 7 feet in length, which is what had led his wife to assume it had merely been a black bear on all-fours. Now, however, they could see that it was closer to 30 feet long, and appeared to resemble either a giant snake or a monstrous eel.

Both of the Shaw's confirmed to me that the creature seemed to have great trouble moving on land, hence their "shuffling" description, to which they added that it seemed to "wriggle from side to side" as it moved, while its body appeared to be "continually vibrating" as it did so. They were unable to discern the nature of the beast's head, said Jeff Shaw, adding, "the whole thing reminded us of a big black pipe."

The Shaw's stated that they did not feel frightened in the presence of the unknown creature, only awe-struck. And while they did not actually see it enter the waters of Lake Klamath, they were sure that this was its ultimate destination. At no time did it make any noise as it passed by, said the couple, and it appeared not to notice them in the slightest. On the following two days they returned to the same spot, hoping to see the remarkable animal once again, and Jeff Shaw even camped out one night near the water's edge, hoping for a truly close encounter. It was unfortunately (or fortunately, depending on your perspective) not to be, however. Whatever the true nature of the beast, it summarily failed to appear again for Jeff Shaw and his wife. The waters of Lake Klamath continued—and continue to this day—to keep a tight grip on their dark secrets, it would appear.

The Shaw's story was very interesting to me for one, key reason: While living back in England in the late 1980s, I had actually heard, on at least three previous occasions, impressive stories of large eels that had allegedly been seen in the winding canals of the English city of Birmingham, and certain areas of the nearby county of Staffordshire, from the mid-to-late 1970s onward. So, in other words, the Shaw's account was not so strange at all.

One particularly memorable tale had come from a truck driver who recalled such a sighting somewhere in Birmingham in the late 1980s, and that "shook the staff rigid" at a building that overlooked the stretch of canal in question. In this case, the animal was described as being dark brown in color and was said to be no less than

15 feet in length. Supposedly, it had been briefly seen on a sunny day by a fork-lift driver, who had sat, utterly mesmerized, watching it "circling" one particular area of the canal that was frequented by a large number of semi-tame ducks, which the staff in question would regularly feed during their lunch hour. Similar to the beast viewed briefly by the Shaw's back in 1969, it vanished without trace, never again to return to haunt the canals of Birmingham.

In the early part of 2003, the author Ryan Wood phoned me and explained that he had decided to hold a conference in Las Vegas in November of that same year on the controversial subject of crashed UFOs. He envisaged making it a yearly event (which it subsequently did become—and a highly successful one, too), where those with a particular interest in crashed UFO stories could gather and learn the latest on the notorious Roswell incident of July 1947, the alien autopsy film, *Area 51*, and much more.

Ryan asked me, "Do you have any ideas as to who we can get on board to speak at the conference?" I did, indeed. After getting off the phone with Ryan, I quickly called one of my oldest and closest mates, who was also the leading light in Britain's monster-hunting community: Jon Downes. In 1998, Jon and a colleague, Graham Inglis, had traveled deep into the heart of Puerto Rico in search of a weird, vampire-like beast alleged by many to resemble a diabolical cross between a monkey, a hyena, a gargoyle, and a stereotypical, black-eyed, bald-headed alien, which would become universally known as the Chupacabras.

The Chupacabras had little—if, indeed, anything—to do with crashed UFOs. I knew, however, that while he was on the island hunting the monster, Jon had uncovered numerous tales of a conspiratorial nature relating to a crashed UFO incident that had reportedly occurred deep within the darkened depths of Puerto Rico's El Yunque rain forest at some not-entirely-determined point in the mid-1980s. Could Jon present a picture-driven lecture that would reveal the facts to what would hopefully be a wide-eyed and awestruck audience?

"Of course I can, dear boy!" he bellowed down the phone. So, the game was well and truly afoot, as Holmes would remark to Watson.

While everyone else, myself included, I confess, gave long-winded lectures on everything of a strictly crashed UFO nature, Jon instead elected to spend his time busily telling the bemused audience about the sexual activities of the island's lesser-spotted great newt—or some such similarly weird creature, anyway—and the delights of Puerto Rican cuisine. Finally, he did get around to the crashed UFO story, but I forget now what all the fuss was about. I do recall, however, that it involved an unidentified flying object that had allegedly slammed into the ground in a particular part of the El Yunque rain forest, as well as tales of the removal by that same U.S. military of the object and its crew of diminutive, bald-headed, black-eyed aliens. The usual *X-Files* stuff, in other words.

Two days later, the conference was well and truly over, and Jon and I were sitting in the departure lounge of Las Vegas's McCarran Airport. Jon had decided to stay in the United States for an extra week, and so he flew back to Nederland with me, where he hung out with me and Dana for the next seven days, merrily eating gumbo and rampaging wildly around darkened woods in hot pursuit of the Texas Bigfoot. But the journey back to Nederland was not the uneventful trip that we had envisioned. I suppose we should have guessed: Nothing in our lives was ever uneventful.

As soon as we got to our gate for the flight that was scheduled for 1:15 p.m., we learned to our dismay that it had been delayed due to bad weather near Houston Airport. As the day progressed, the delays got longer and sheer boredom began to set in; so, Jon and I decided to play a little game. Every time someone sat next to us, Jon would pull out his cell phone, put on a pair of wrap-around sun glasses, turn up the collar of his dark jacket, and look around the room in a distinctly cloak-and-dagger fashion, and whisper into his phone just loud enough for the person to hear him say: "Condition red, condition red. The Black Condor has landed. I repeat: The Black Condor has landed. Alert all personnel to move in, and terminate with extreme prejudice."

It was my job to judge the reaction of the person who was the subject of our utterly mindless games. Invariably, we were treated with looks of disgust. Doubtless they were not amused by the sight of two men, one in his 30s (me), and the other in his 40s (Jon) playing completely inane, but highly entertaining, games when they really should by now have grown out of such nonsense. The tiring and stressed-out world of adulthood and the attendant responsibilities of kids, mortgages, real jobs, and other such utterly mystifying oddities were not for us, however.

As the cell phone caper continued and the hours rolled by, occasionally we would lure in some unsuspecting and gullible soul who fell for our prank. Distinctly worried, furtive looks would be cast in our direction, whispered conversations with their partners would inevitably and invariably follow, and they would then slowly get up and move to another seat, while still watching us intently. But finally, even we got bored and laid the Black Condor to rest.

Five hours after we were originally due to fly, we were still stuck at the accursed airport. Then, at 7 p.m., an announcement was made that the weather had improved slightly near Houston, and a decision had been made by the captain "to attempt the flight." It was that particularly unusual phraseology that caused many people within the terminal to take on worried frowns. And it was certainly not unwarranted. As we took off from Vegas around 9 p.m. that night, everything started fine, and Jon and I settled back into our respective seats, ate a pleasant chicken dinner, and downed a plentiful supply of drinks. But as the aircraft neared the Texas border, the weather began to get steadily worse again, to the point where we were literally being buffeted around the sky; lightning, thunder, and driving rain became our constant, and only, companions.

On two occasions, at least, the interior lights momentarily went out—amid hysterical screams that emanated from all around the aircraft—and the ominous creaking and groaning of metal could be heard from time to time. Jon closed his eyes tight and began to pray out loud to a whole assortment of deities. But it was his bellowing plea to "the beasts of old England" to get us on the ground in one piece that really shook up the people that were seated across the aisle from us. Here we were, 40,000 feet in the air, in the middle of probably the worst flight that most of us had ever experienced in our lives, and Jon was invoking shadowy beings from Britain's dark forests in an admittedly heroic attempt to assist the captain and crew as they struggled valiantly to keep the plane in the air, and subsequently get us on the ground in one piece. And finally, we *were* on the ground—and in that much-welcome one piece, too. In a fashion comically similar to one of those old aircraft disaster movies of the 1970s, everyone cheered and clapped when we finally came to a screeching, bouncing halt, and we all disembarked; many I suspect, with distinctly shaky legs.

But we were still not quite out of the woods: I phoned Dana when we finally got off the plane around midnight, and she told me that numerous trees had come down on the main highway to Houston from Nederland, and the road was blocked. Not only that, but the ongoing storm meant that countless trees were still coming down, so I told her not to even attempt the 90-minute car journey alone at the witching hour. Instead, Jon and I settled down in the terminal for a night on the floor, with our carry-on luggage substituting for pillows. It was a torturous seven hours. But dawn finally broke, and after a Mexican breakfast we got a ride to Nederland,

and were soon sprawled on our living room couch devouring gumbo and indulging in a fine bottle of red wine.

It was the first time that Jon and Dana had seen each other since her visit to England in May 2001, and we had a good old time catching up on gossip and telling stories, while Charity sniffed, and stared intently at, her grizzly-bear-like visitor from across the ocean. The next day, I drove Jon, with Charity pacing and panting excitedly on the back seat, around the swamps in search of alligators, snakes, and road-kill—and, fortunately, he got to see and photograph all three. But it was the following day that, I suspect, was Jon's favorite.

Only a few miles from Nederland was the town of Orange, where renowned cryptozoologist Chester Moore lived. I had first first Chester in the summer of 2003 at his Crypto Conference in Conroe, Texas. Several days before I flew to Vegas, I had phoned Chester to tell him that Jon was finally coming over, and he was eager to arrange a meeting. So, I called Chester again, and he drove over, and Jon and I spent the day with him exploring the woods of East Texas and visiting various places where giant, hairy behemoths had been seen roaming—and by that I do not mean Jon. But first we paid a visit to Chester's home, where he showed us around his office, which was packed with Bigfoot footprint casts, cryptozoology-related movie posters, and, incredibly, a life-sized replica of Bigfoot himself that Chester had christened "Boggy." The model had apparently gotten its name from the 1973 movie, *The Legend of Boggy Creek*, which told the story of a series of bizarre man-beast encounters in the early 1970s in Fouke, Arkansas.

Seeing Jon stand next to the beast, as I took a few photographs, momentarily flummoxed me, as the resemblance between the two was uncannily remarkable. Indeed, they could have almost been twins, I thought to myself. But then it was time to hit the road.

The good thing about investigating monsters in East Texas is the fact that a person does not have to venture far off the main highways before they are deep into the woods. And having done so, Chester told us some amazing stories about the unholy sounds (or "vocalizations" as he preferred it) that he had heard from within the dense trees late at night, which he was firmly convinced originated with the creature known as Bigfoot. Footprints abounded, he said, and there was no doubt that something monstrous was lurking inside those sinister woods.

We didn't find the creature, mind you, but having seen the thick, practically impenetrable forestland for ourselves, both Jon and I were firmly convinced of the veracity and credibility of Chester's research. After Chester dropped us off back at our house, we said our collective goodbyes, and then with Dana, we headed out for an evening of fine food, finer wine, and good conversation. And then, after a couple of more days of relaxation it was time for Jon to begin his long journey back to his English home, and for me and Dana to plan our next adventure—a move to the big city of Dallas. But not before I had chance to speak with a man who claimed a truly startling, decades-old close encounter of the werewolf kind in the exact same woods in which Jon and I had roamed with Chester mere days before.

Solomon's story was a highly intriguing one because it involved the sighting of a mysterious beast that seemed to eerily fit the pattern of the classic shapeshifting werewolf with which Hollywood movie-makers have for so long been enamored. In his mid-80s at the time I spoke with him, Solomon still retained all of his faculties, and had both a sharp mind and a keen wit. And to his credit, Solomon realized that the controversial nature of his story was one that would surely make some people wonder if he had lost his mind. He assured me on several occasions that he had not.

Solomon's encounter had occurred in the woods near Orange in 1933—a full 70 years before we spoke, and at which time he was in his mid-teens. He told me in graphic detail of how he had spent most of one particular Sunday morning in the early part of the year in question exploring the woods with a couple of friends, and fishing in several small pools that they happened to stumble upon. By noon, the trio of adventurers had retreated to the edge of a winding stream that cut through the woods, and sat and ate a small lunch that his mother had thoughtfully prepared for them.

The friendly chatter of Solomon and his two friends came to an ominous halt, however, when all three of them suddenly developed an ominous feeling of "being watched." Indeed, they were. Upon glancing across the stream they were shocked and terror-stricken to see a huge wolf-like head partly protruding from out of the dense undergrowth. And, explained Solomon, when the beast "realized we had seen it," it emerged fully from its hiding place and "paced along the edge of the water, one way then the other, five or six times."

And while the creature was certainly wolf-like in its appearance, in no way could it be considered a conventional one. Rather, explained Solomon, the creature was quite literally a monster: easily 10 feet in length, it appeared to be incredibly powerful, and possessed huge, muscular limbs, a very thick neck, an overly elongated jaw, and a "hump on the top of his neck." While keeping Solomon and his friends in sight at all times, the nightmarish beast issued forth a continuous guttural growl and occasionally wrinkled its jaw, as if poised to launch an attack. Yet, no such attack came. However, something else occurred that, in many ways, Solomon said was even more frightening.

After a few minutes, Solomon told me, the animal "sat down" and "started to shake." It was at this point that matters became distinctly surreal. The creature, that was undoubtedly four-legged in nature, became enveloped in a slight "green fog" that lasted for but a moment, and then suddenly reared up on to its hind-legs. Still definitively wolf-like in appearance, its stance was now that of a large man, or perhaps that of the classic werewolf of folklore would be more accurate.

Interestingly, Solomon said that he got the distinct impression that the creature meant him and his friends no physical harm as such, but seemed to achieve a perverse delight and satisfaction in scaring the boys out of their collective wits. For perhaps 20 seconds, the mighty creature—which, having adopted an upright stance, seemed even bigger than it had while walking on four legs—snarled and snapped in what was perceived as a malevolent, hostile, and even sinister fashion. Most bizarre of all was the fact that the paws of the creature appeared to have shapeshifted into large, man-like hands, albeit a pair covered in a thick coating of hair. Then, without warning, the animal turned and headed into the dense trees, looking back in the direction of the boys only once, and just before it finally disappeared.

Not surprisingly, the stunned trio exited the woods at high speed and breathlessly headed for Solomon's home. The boys decided not to tell anyone of their unearthly encounter, probably correctly assuming that they would "get a whipping" for making up fantastic tales. Nevertheless, Solomon was adamant that his story was completely and utterly true, and added to me that he had far better things to do with his remaining years on this Earth than make up bizarre tales about werewolves.

So, what was it that Solomon and his two friends had seen on that long gone Sunday back in 1933? While the seemingly shapeshifting nature of the beast and the presence of the "green fog" strongly suggested to me a paranormal point of origin, there were other possibilities. Werewolf hunter Linda Godfrey, who I had interviewed earlier, had suggested that at least some of the creatures perceived as werewolves, seen in the forests and woods of the United States, might actually be surviving relics of beasts collectively known as *Amphicyonidae*, or "dogs of doubtful origin."

A fierce combination of large bear and muscular dog, one such creature that fell into this category was the *Amphicyon*, a powerful, imposing, and deadly creature that lived in the Miocene era, some 23 to 25 million years ago, after which time it became extinct. Or perhaps it would be more correct to say that it is *assumed* it became extinct. Was it possible that a group of such animals still inhabited the many thick woods and forests of the United States as late as 1933—and perhaps even today? Possibly—however, what about the seemingly paranormal aspects of the affair?

Linda Godfrey made an important statement that may go some way toward providing an explanation. Commenting on similar creatures seen in her home state of Wisconsin, she said: "Native Americans believe that each animal has a 'master spirit' responsible for maintaining survival. Could the master spirit of the *Amphicyon* still walk the northern Wisconsin woods, searching for its long-lost corporeal cousins?"

I had no idea; however, while it was completely unforeseen to me at the time, not longer after speaking with Solomon my relationship to the twilight world of animal spirits would increase dramatically—and tragically, too.

7

Spectral Animals

As our time in Nederland drew to a close, Dana and I were upbeat about our planned relocation to Dallas in January 2004. But with the old year almost over, and as we began the pain-in-the-neck-task of packing, we could scarcely have imagined that our relocation would be overshadowed by complete and utter tragedy. On two occasions in the preceding six weeks we had had to take our dog, Charity, to the veterinarians when her pulse rate and temperature both soared, and her breathing had become extremely labored. At first, there was nothing but puzzlement and alarm on the part of the doctors. But it would later become apparent that she was suffering from something known as Familial Shar-Pei Fever, a hereditary and sometimes fatal condition caused by in-bred shar-peis that not only includes joint pain and accompanied physical distress, but also bouts of sudden fevers up to an alarming 107 degrees. Thankfully, after each of the two attacks Charity's doctor managed to lower her temperature, and with a variety of medications, succeeded in returning her to her normal, fun-loving self. But, sadly, time was no longer on her side.

It was a Saturday on the first weekend of December 2003, and being a gloriously sunny day, Dana and I decided to take Charity for a walk around a nearby park that we visited occasionally. I still vividly recall how, as the sun shone down on us and as the birds sang and whistled, we ran and ran, while Charity seized the lead in her powerful jaws and shook it vigorously—which she always did when overwhelming excitement kicked in on those long walks and

Charity, our dog who came back from the grave.

runs. Charity spun around in circles wildly as we raced along, practically pulling my arm out of its socket as she ran me, rather than the other way around. Occasionally, she would come to a sudden halt when she smelled something that had caught her attention, and she would head for the bushes, snorting in the process as she sought out her quarry. After about three quarters of an hour we drove home, and all seemed fine. Charity bounded into the house, lapped up half a bowl of water, and contentedly went to sleep on the cold, stone kitchen tiles.

That night, however, was a strange one. We settled back to watch *Final Destination 2* on video, a movie that told the story of a group of people who had cheated death—until death came looking for them. Halfway through the movie, I went to the refrigerator to grab a drink and noticed that the interior light was not working. I walked over to a cupboard where the bulbs were stored, took one out, and headed back to the refrigerator. I was about to place the new bulb in its rightful position when I noticed that the area surrounding the light socket was soaked in water. I pulled back just in time to prevent what could have been a very nasty electric shock. For a brief moment a weird feeling came over me, and I actually felt like a very real Reaper was among us, ready to take a soul in the fashion very similar to that which was being portrayed on our TV set at that very moment. I might not have been wrong.

On the following morning, Sunday, we awoke around 9 a.m. and Charity was standing in the doorway looking at us. Normally, she would rouse us by jumping on the bed in her usual boisterous fashion, so we called her, but she did not budge. Something was not right. We got out of bed and bent down beside her and could see that her legs were slightly swollen. Dana and I looked at each other. We knew exactly what it was: another attack of Familial Shar-Pei Fever. The veterinarian had told us that if she had a future attack, in the short term, half an aspirin could prove helpful. So we gave that to her and she seemed to improve as the day progressed. But early on the Monday morning, she seemed slightly worse, and so I drove immediately to the veterinarian's office, waited for the staff to arrive, and explained the situation. The nurse asked me: "Have you ever given a dog a shot?" As it transpired, I had. Back in England, in early 1993, my pet terrier Susie developed diabetes, and I had to learn to give her insulin injections twice a day, until her death in 1998, at the age of nearly 19. He quickly gave me a syringe and a plentiful supply of medication, and I sped back to the house. Within a few hours Charity seemed much better, and even ate a small amount of food. But that night she deteriorated and by morning began to vomit.

We wasted no time and drove Charity to the veterinarian's office at lightning speed. By the time we arrived, she was even worse: her breathing was very shallow and she could barely walk. The doctor and nurse quickly got her on to an operating table and hooked her up to an IV. "Is she going to die?" Dana asked with tears flowing in her eyes. Charity's doctor, who had cared for her for all of her eight years, was genuinely worried and replied: "Well, it doesn't look good."

Thankfully, however, after an hour or two of medication she seemed to improve, and later that afternoon she was even able to walk. The staff wanted Charity kept under their watchful eyes, and so that evening we took her to the nearby 24-hour emergency office that worked in conjunction with the vet's office. Unfortunately, in a matter of hours her condition worsened again. But she was still hanging on, and early on the following morning we took her back to the regular clinic where she was due to receive more medication. But things did not look good: Her legs were even more swollen and slightly discolored now, and her breathing was again labored. As I drove, Dana sat in the back of the car with Charity, holding her and gently petting her, as she tried to offer some comfort to our faithful companion.

We left her with the staff that advised us to return home and await their call. Much to our delight, Charity's doctor phoned around 11 a.m. to say that she had made a vast improvement and he was going to let us bring her home around lunchtime. Dana, overjoyed, quickly headed out to do some chores before we drove to collect her, and I returned smiling to my office. About 40 minutes later, the doctor called and said, "Mr. Redfern, I'm sorry to have to tell you that Charity just died." I felt like I had been punched in the chest. As I sat listening, numbly, the doctor told me that she had been fine one minute, but that her heart had apparently just stopped beating. One second she was there, he said, and the next she was gone.

"Gone." It was the utter finality of that word that made me realize we would never play with Charity again. Never again would we run around the block with her, or hear her loud snorting, or the pitter-patter of her claws on the corridor tiles as she headed to our bedroom, as was her regular morning fashion. I sat, head bowed on the couch, thinking that the vet had to have been wrong. Charity couldn't be dead. But I knew she was. Then, 10 minutes later a sound came from the driveway that I dreaded. It was the closing of a car door, and Dana was back. And I had to break the news to her.

Needless to say, Dana was crushed. Utterly crushed. Her best friend was gone, quite literally, in a heartbeat. She broke down and cried and cried. I phoned the veterinarian and made arrangements for us to go down later that afternoon and collect Charity. When we arrived we were motioned through a back door into a small room where the staff had laid Charity in a large basket with a blanket around her. Dana, sobbing uncontrollably, hugged her and I stood around feeling useless and helpless. Even the staff was visibly upset, and particularly so, Charity's doctor who had looked after her for all of her life.

We arranged to return the basket the next day and then phoned Danny and Melissa to break the sad news, and to ask if we could bury Charity on their huge property. Of course Danny said yes. I drove out to their home on Pleasure Island while Dana sat in the back of the car, cradling Charity in her hands. By the time we got out there, the sun was already setting and darkness was falling upon the island. As a result, after finding a nice, peaceful location I maneuvered the car in front of it and turned on the headlights for illumination. Then, having got a shovel from Danny, I began the task of digging into the thick, hard soil. Melissa came out to help—

on what was the night of her birthday, no less—while Dana continued to sit in the back of the car, saying her private goodbyes to Charity.

Having finally laid Charity to rest, we began the long journey home. But this time the drive seemed much longer than normal. We retired to bed and Dana, still crying, said to me: "Momma's baby girl is really gone." I could only nod. She really was. Or was she? Over the course of the next three weeks, and directly up until the time we left for Dallas, some very strange things occurred that made us both think that Charity's life force was still around and that she was not gone, after all.

Although I have a deep and passionate interest in the unexplained, most of that interest is focused upon cryptozoology. Life after death was an issue that I had never personally delved into beyond reading books on the subject and watching the occasional TV documentary. But there were events that I recalled quite vividly. When I was 14, my grandmother on my dad's side of the family died in the hospital. She had been living with us for a while until her condition worsened to the point where there was no choice but to have her hospitalized. I distinctly remember how my mom, on several occasions immediately after my grandmother's death, detected what she believed was her presence in the bedroom where she had stayed in her final months.

I confess, however, that I often wavered on the subject of life after death. There were times when I was a firm believer, other times when I was agnostic, and times I feared that all talk of an afterlife was wishful thinking, and that beyond death there was nothing but endless oblivion. But after Charity's passing, that all changed. And it all began one week after her death, just as we were leaving Danny and Melissa's place after spending the evening with them for dinner.

It was around 9 p.m. and it was pouring rain as we turned out of their drive and onto the highway. As we drove near their long fence line, we drew parallel with Charity's grave and Dana shouted: "Come with us, girl!" We continued the journey and got home about 25 minutes later. We had parked the car in the garage, and went into the house. We were both immediately struck by something: Next to the chair where I always sit was what looked like Charity's imprint—body, legs, and all. She would typically lie there at night, but we had vacuumed the area twice in the week after she had died and the mark that had been there previously was gone. But now it was back. We stared at each other, wondering if this was some sort of sign that Charity was still with us, and this was her way of getting the message across to us.

Then, if that were not enough, at approximately 10:30 p.m., I went into the garage to take some clothes out of the dryer. As I did so, I was hit by what was without doubt the most overpowering odor of wet dog that I have encountered in my life. It was almost as if I had walked into a solid wall. I quickly called Dana, who came running and she, too, was taken aback by the sheer strength of the odor. Given that this had occurred on the same rainy night that Dana had beckoned Charity's spirit to "come with us," this was decidedly odd, and I confess that I was both amazed and slightly shocked by the events. But things did not end there.

During the course of the next couple of days, Charity's unmistakable odor returned, at various times and in several locations, including the bathroom adjacent to our bedroom where Charity never entered. Late at night several days later, Dana had heard what sounded like the pitter-patter of Charity's claws on the corridor tiles, as if she was heading toward our bedroom, and as she would sometimes do in the middle of the night, particularly if she had been spooked by a powerful thunderstorm.

Then, on the following morning I had a highly strange dream. Indeed, it was so graphic and unusual that it seemed to be more than an average dream. In fact, I was sure that it was some form of supernatural contact. In the dream, I had heard our doorbell ring loudly, and then saw Charity and my old dog from England, Susie, running down the corridor and jumping on our bed. Susie seemed different, however, and rather like a wise, ancient figure. But Charity was her usual excitable, chaotic self, bumping into things and bouncing around the bed and overjoyed to be home. I reached out to stroke them both and as I did so, I could not help but notice that their texture was different: very hard and solid. Suddenly, they vanished and I awoke. Was it all a dream, a form of wishful thinking borne out of an unconscious wish to have Charity and Susie back? Considering the high-strangeness and clarity of the events, I concluded that it was far more than a mere dream. But the weirdest thing of all occurred on the day we left town in late January 2004 to start a new life in Dallas.

Given the fact that it seemed to both of us that Charity's spirit was still with us, Dana was very upset that, as we prepared to leave Nederland, the dog's life force would remain at our old house, forever trapped within its confines and unable to leave. We both concentrated hard and sent out a message for her to leave as well. It was around midday when we were finally ready to go. Everything was loaded onto a huge truck and, once again, we were bound for a new destination.

I said to Dana only minutes before we were due to leave that I would have one last look around the house—just to make sure we hadn't left anything behind. I checked each room and all of the cupboards but found nothing. The last room I checked was my office, where I spent my weekdays working, and where Charity would lie, sprawled across the carpet, snoring, or happily eating pieces of bread that I would toss in her direction.

I looked around the room: nothing. I then checked the closet where I used to store some of my files and jumped into the air to have a look on the top of a shelf that ran the length of the closet. As I did so, I noticed something small and dark on the shelf. I jumped again and grabbed it with my hand. I was amazed to find that it was a small negative of a photograph of Charity, staring intently at the camera, that had been taken in 2001 in Alex and Gloria's backyard at Littlefield. Considering that I had gone back into the house to make sure that we had not left anything behind, I took this to be a symbolic message that Charity would be on her way soon, too, and that this was her way of getting the message across.

After having told this to Dana, who expressed both joy and amazement, I made a quick journey to the local McDonalds to get us a couple of chocolate shakes. While I was away, Dana sat on the driveway, having one last look around the neighborhood. She was fiddling with her tennis shoes, and pulled on a label that was affixed to one of them. Its logo read: *Time to get moving*. Stuck to the label was one of Charity's hairs. Moved to tears, she told me when I returned with the drinks how she was now certain that, collectively the startling events of the last few weeks were all evidence that Charity's spirit was still with us. This, said Dana, was an indication that just as it was time for us to leave, it was time for Charity to go, too. And the dog was letting us know, in her own unique way, that it was okay for us to move on with our lives. We jumped into the truck, I turned on the ignition, and we headed out of Nederland bound for a new life. We were certain that Charity was about to begin a new life, too.

Sure enough, after our move to Dallas, neither of us, sadly, ever got another indication of Charity's presence among us. But the strangeness was still not quite over. I have a friend from San Diego named Eric who is a strong adherent of Buddhist teachings, and who spends a lot of time in Tibet. I e-mailed him when we got to Dallas and told him of our experiences after Charity's death. Eric, in turn, relayed me a synchronistic tale about how, shortly before I had contacted him, he had dreamed of a dog barking, which for some reason had stuck firmly in his mind. As he was in Tibet at the time, Eric blessed a Tibetan sacred prayer cloth, known as a Kharta, for Charity, and said a prayer for her. At the time, Eric did not know that Charity was a shar-pei. But when I told him, he considered it to be highly synchronistic, considering the breed's Asian origins, that he had made the blessing in Tibet.

Four years after Charity's death, Dana and I have not gotten a new dog, and neither do we particularly want one. We still miss her, and not a week goes by that we do not think about the big lug, or talk about her and her antics. Even though I did not know Charity as a puppy, I am very glad that I got to spend three years with her. She was a kind and fun-loving dog, with a unique character all of her own. And neither Dana nor I will ever forget her or stop loving her, wherever she may be now. I admit that I have no clear idea what happens to us after death, only that it is not the end of the adventure. It may just be the beginning. And I have a dog to thank for finally and firmly convincing me of that. So, Charity, in whatever twilight realm you now inhabit, I hope you are still looking down on us, and waiting patiently for the day when all three of us will be reunited. Until then, I'm sure you're causing as much rambunctious, fun-packed chaos there as you did in your eight years on Earth.

8

Creatures of the Black Lagoon

Our new abode, which was destined to be our home for almost two years, was a pleasant third-floor apartment at a gated complex that was situated practically on the shores of Dallas's White Rock Lake, a picturesque and tree-shrouded area that was tucked away only a few miles outside of the city's downtown. But just like everywhere we seemed to go, White Rock Lake had a distinctly strange atmosphere, and it was an atmosphere that just got stranger and stranger as time progressed. Legends of monstrous fish, bizarre man-beasts, the Lady of the Lake, deranged killers, and wartime Nazi spies all emanated from the heart of White Rock Lake. Oh, and nothing less than an island had mysteriously gone missing from within its murky waters.

Constructed in 1911 as Dallas's first reservoir, White Rock Lake has 9 1/2 miles of shoreline, thick trees, a path for walkers and cyclists, and is home to an estimated 33 types of mammals, including squirrels, rabbits, skunks, raccoons, possums, bobcats, red foxes, and minks, and no less than 54 varieties of reptiles, among which are rattlesnakes, turtles, a whole variety of lizards, and horned toads. Salamanders and frogs also abound, along with an incredible 217 species of bird, including swans, pelicans, sea gulls, loons, and all manner of ducks.

As I got to know some of the elderly locals, a number of whom had been there since the 1930s, I learned that the tale of the Lady of the Lake had been circulating for years. As the story went, a Dr. Eckersall, a local physician, was driving home from a country-club dance late one Saturday night when he saw a young girl by the lake, who he suspected was in trouble. He quickly stopped his car, and motioned her to climb into the back seat of his vehicle.

"Please, please take me home," she begged. The doctor drove quickly to her destination, and as he pulled up before the shuttered house, he said: "Here we are." Then he turned around. Yep, you guessed it: The back seat was empty, except for a small puddle of lake water dripping down onto the floorboard. He thought for a moment then rang insistently on the house bell. Finally the door was opened by a gray-haired man.

"I can't tell you what an amazing thing has happened," began the doctor, breathlessly. "A young girl gave me this address. I drove her here and..."

"Yes, yes, I know," the man wearily interrupted. "This has happened several other Saturday evenings in the past month. That young girl, sir, was my daughter. She was killed in a boating accident on White Rock Lake almost two years ago."

Needless to say, this was a tale I was very pleased to get my teeth into. And like a lot of such tales, there were many rumors but very few facts. The late writer and researcher Ed Syers said:

> In the 1920s, an excursion boat operated on the lake. One warm summer night, perfect for a moonlit ride, a young couple attended a formal party on the boat. An argument between the lovers ensued—possibly alcohol-induced—and the woman left the boat, jumped into her date's car, and sped off into the dark night. The poorly maintained road around the lake twisted and turned, and the distraught woman lost control of the car where Lawther Road runs into Garland Road. The car careened into the lake and she drowned.

This was particularly interesting to me as our apartment complex was on Garland Road, so I continued to dig into the tales. According to acclaimed Austin, Texas-based ghost hunter Lisa Farwell:

> One of the scariest reports of the ghost appeared in a 1987 *Dallas Times Herald* article by Lorraine Iannello. Iannello interviewed a mother and daughter, Phyllis Thompson and Sue Ann Ashman, who had a frightening encounter with the female phantom. The two were

> sitting on one of the boat docks at night when they spotted a white object floating in the lake. The women heard a blood-curdling scream and saw the white object roll over onto its back. The object turned out to be a body; it stared at the horror-stricken women through big, hollow sockets where the eyes should have been. Then, just as quickly, the terrifying sight disappeared.

Interestingly, a perusal of old newspapers revealed to me that, in the late 1970s, the story of a woman who was claiming to be the "real" Lady of the Lake surfaced briefly in an article written by Dallas Morning News columnist John Anders. According to Anders, the woman had written to the newspaper describing how, on one night back in the 1930s she and her lover were parked by the lake, watching a full moon. While they sat together, however, the man's car suddenly rolled into the lake, its parking brake presumably having failed. Dripping wet, she hitched a ride to her parents' house on Gaston Avenue. And sure enough, the legend of the mysterious drowned lady started soon afterward. The woman cryptically signed her note "Jam Net Jaid," taunting Anders to figure out her real identity. She remained elusive. But the one case of the Lady of the Lake that I personally investigated turned out to be truly creepy.

After we moved to White Rock, I was interviewed by a local magazine that specifically served East Dallas. The feature, titled *In Search of Sasquatch*, had been written by the magazine's editor Kris Scott, and brought me a lot of local attention and also, and more importantly, a lot of stories and leads to follow up on. And one such story, from Bobby John Craig, had a direct bearing on the ghostly woman of the lake. Craig's family was originally from Tulsa, Oklahoma, but had moved to Texas in the 1960s. And as a lifelong fisherman, Craig had fished White Rock Lake for many years.

As I listened, Craig told me a macabre tale about the fateful night he sat on the far side of the lake in 1971. It was a summer's evening and he had been fishing for a while, with considerable success, when he was overcome by an all-encompassing feeling of dread, and saw something slowly begin to haul itself out of the water about 20 feet in front of him. To his horror, he could see that it was a woman—or perhaps some insane soul's monstrous and diabolical idea of what a woman should look like would be a better description.

Craig told me that the woman was dressed in dark rags, had long black hair, deathly white skin, and her soulless eyes were utterly jet-black. Dirty water dripped from her mud-encrusted locks, and she moved slowly toward him with a maniacal grin on her face. Her slow, jerky fashion reminded Craig of the relentless flesh-eating zombies that were featured in George A. Romero's classic movie *Night of the Living Dead*. The creature—it may have looked human, said Craig, but a creature is all it really was—continued to move toward him in faltering steps, its arms outstretched, while it issued a dark and sinister moan and pointed an elongated finger in his direction. This was enough to convince Craig to grab his rod and gear, and hit the road, which he duly did.

On the following day, and after the shock had worn off, Craig tentatively revisited the site of his unearthly encounter. The woman was gone. And despite the fact that Craig continued to fish that same area for several more years, he never saw the horrific specter again. But there were far stranger things than weird, wet women afoot at White Rock.

White Rock Lake: home to giant catfish and marauding man-beasts.

One story that really did make me wonder was that of the lake's Men in Black. During the Second World War, White Rock Lake had been used as a camp for German prisoners-of-war that had been captured from General Erwin Rommel's Afrika Corps. Inevitably, anxious neighbors frequently reported to the FBI suspicious men they feared were prisoners attempting to escape, but apparently there was never anything concrete about the rumors.

However, Ernie Sanders, another source who had contacted me in the wake of the Advocate's article, told me a controversial story that, if true, may still be considered classified by the government.

It was 1944 and the Second World War was at its height. Sanders, however, was exempt from military service due to the loss of a leg as a child, but was employed as a cartographer for "a civilian agency that worked with the military." As a direct result of his work, Sanders had learned from a colleague, a woman who lived on the lake, that she had seen several strange characters on at least three occasions roaming around late at night, stealthily taking photographs of the area and the surrounding houses, and generally acting very odd. Dressed in trench coats with turned-up collars and pulled-down hats, they resembled what could best be described as a combination of classic 1940s era G-Man, gangster, and gumshoe detective. But what was going on? Who were the mysterious figures? What was so important about their mission that it required them to walk the lake after darkness had fallen? And more importantly, what were the strange and powerful lights that she had seen emanating from the center of the White Rock Lake at around 2 a.m. the previous Saturday?

It transpired that Sanders learned—but declined to say precisely how he had learned—that all of the weird activity was due to the fact that the military was testing a very small and portable submersible in White Rock Lake. Its shape was rather similar to a missile, in which a man would lay flat and steer the device with his feet. Supposedly on the third test, a calamity of unprecedented proportions occurred when the device suddenly sunk into the depths of the lake without warning. Unfortunately, it was pitch black, and the mini-sub dropped like a stone, ensuring "the pilot," as Sanders described him, a certain and nightmarish death within the cramped confines of the metal tomb.

Of course, ultimately locating the device was not too much of a problem, and it was undertaken by a team of divers who were on standby near the shore with a small rowboat. Despite the fact that the team raced out to the approximate location, the crewman had already drowned. Worse news followed: The recovery of the device was witnessed by an elderly man doing a bit of late-night fishing on the lake. He was ordered, at gunpoint, to the shore where he was asked in a stern fashion: "Who are you? What are you doing on the lake? And where do you live?" The plan was to merely put the fear of God into the fisherman and explain to him that it was his patriotic duty to remain silent. All would have gone smoothly except for the fact that within 10 minutes of being scared out of his wits by big and burly G-Men, spooks, and MPs, the man was suddenly taken ill and died on the shore of the lake, presumably of a stress-induced heart attack.

This created a real quandary, said Sanders, and so a hasty plan was put into action. The man's body was loaded onto a military jeep, and taken to downtown Dallas where it was dumped in a fashion that made it look as if the unfortunate man had died in the street, or as if he had been the victim of a vicious attack. In fact, to reinforce this latter scenario, the G-Men emptied his wallet of money and threw it on the ground near to his body, confident that whoever found it would assume that the man's death was indeed robbery-related. Sanders presumed that the ruse worked, and the disturbing affair was successfully buried by a highly concerned military.

Was the story true, was it a friend-of-a-friend tale, or was it merely the ramblings of an old man? I was never certain, but if Sanders was not being earnest and honest, then he deserved an Oscar, to be sure. White Rock Lake, it seemed, was just full of secrets and strangeness. And it might have been full of gargantuan fish, too.

Phil Groff told me a notable story of a very large catfish that he estimated to be in excess of an incredible 200 pounds, and which he saw in the summer of 1979 while rowing across the lake. Too amazed to do anything but stare in awe for the several seconds that the majestic creature was in view, Groff watched the great beast sink beneath the waves, never to resurface. Like a real-life Captain Ahab, an obsessed Groff took his boat onto the lake for years afterward, in the hope of once again seeing the mighty fish. But it was all to no avail. The leviathan forever eluded him. But White Rock Lake's monsters of the deep extended far beyond overweight catfish.

In early 2005, I drove to Austin, Texas, to meet with Rob Riggs and a friend of his, Mike, to discuss some potential television work. As we sat and ate lunch, I was astonished to learn from Mike that he had a friend (not a friend-of-a-friend, I hasten to add) who knew of a baby alligator that had been secretly released into the heart of the lake some years previously. Was the beast now fully grown, and marauding wildly within its murky depths? I actually hoped it was, as it would be a great story if true, albeit not for anyone that happened to have the bad luck to get in the way of its bone-crushing jaws. Perhaps they needed to change the lake's name to Lake Placid, I thought to myself.

The most notable resident monster of White Rock Lake, however, was the ludicrously named Goat-Man. Alligator Man would have been cool, as would have Shark Man, or even Snake Man. But Goat-Man's moniker most certainly was not. So the story went, on several occasions in the 1970s and 1980s a distinctly odd creature was seen flitting in and out of the trees after sunset, was described as being man-like in form, around 7 feet in height, but with Goat-style protrusions sticking out of its head, and hooves instead of feet. The description of the animal was eerily like that of the fabled Satyrs of Greek and Roman legend. And it must be noted that numerous other cultures had an awareness of such strange creatures lurking among them. There was, for example, the demon goat-man Azazel, the goat-beast of the mountains that was feared by the herdsmen of Parnassus, and, of course, there was the god Pan.

The deity of woods and fields, and of flocks and shepherds, Pan dwelt in grottos, roamed both mountains and valleys, was a lover of music, and was universally feared. In ancient days, any form of overwhelming dread without a discernible cause was ascribed to Pan, and became known as a Panic terror. Pan came to be considered a symbol of the universe and the personification of

Nature; and was almost certainly the inspiration for the Latin divinities, Sylvanus and Faunus.

Rob Riggs wrote briefly about the Goat-Man sightings at White Rock Lake in the book Weird Texas; the details, however, were scant. But a far more substantial account was brought to my attention by Sandy Grace, who had seen the Goat-Man, up close and personal, in August 2001. Grace had been jogging around the lake on the 9-mile-long trail at around 2 p.m. when, out of the trees, she told me, stepped the strangest looking thing she had ever seen. Large, and covered in thin, coarse brown hair with two large horn-like protrusions, the half-man-half-beast strode purposefully in her direction with a malevolent, sneering grin on its face. Bizarrely, when it got within about 15 feet of the terror-stricken Grace, the animal crouched on its four limbs and vanished in a flash of light. She was sure that it had not been a hallucination, but was equally sure that such a thing could not live within the confines of White Rock Lake—or indeed anywhere on the face of the Earth.

Interestingly, Grace told me that about a minute or so before the Goat-Man appeared, she was overcome by an intense feeling of fear, albeit for no particular reason. She had never suffered from panic attacks (before or since), but figured that that was probably the best way to describe how she felt. I thought to myself that it could also have been a classic description of an encounter with Pan, the God of the Woods, centuries ago. And as I related earlier, induced states of panic in people was the veritable calling card of the Cormons of old England.

Was it only a coincidence that cultures all around the world in times past had legends and tales of such creatures inhabiting dark woods and forests, and that, today, people were still seeing them in similar locations? I concluded that it most certainly was not a coincidence. Something diabolical really was among us. Notably, White Rock Lake was not the only place in Texas that was allegedly inhabited by such a Goat-like man (or a man-like Goat, depending on one's perspective), as I learned graphically in 2005, and as will become apparent in a later chapter.

And then, just when I thought that things could not possibly get any stranger, there was the tale of the vanishing island of White Rock Lake. Could it really be that a small piece of land on the lake, known as Bonnie Bell Island, had vanished into thin air? Well, not quite. There was a smidgen of truth to the tale, however, in a roundabout way, at least. On September 7, 2002, the Dallas Morning News's Larry Bleberg had reported that the online mapping service, Mapquest, had recently dropped from its map of White Rock Lake the aforementioned Bonnie Bell Island. The problem, however, was that the island had never been there in the first place. Rather, it was a deliberate fabrication cooked up by other mapmakers in an ingenious attempt to identify and foil copyright infringement. Incredibly, it was revealed by the newspaper that, at the time, every computerized car navigation system in the United States displayed this real-life fantasy island.

I had to conclude that it was indeed highly appropriate that a strange lake full of monstrous fish, alligators, and a diabolical Goat-Man should also be home to a computer-generated, nonexistent island.

9

In Search of Vampires

It was mid-afternoon in late April 2004. I was sitting, sprawled in my office chair, musing upon how I could convince *Fortean Times* magazine to buy a story from me on crashed UFOs, when the telephone rang. At the other end of the line, a voice identified itself as belonging to a researcher with a television show titled *Proof Positive*, that was then in the preproduction stage for the Sci Fi Channel. He had gotten my name from Kelly McPherson, the producer of a show that I had worked on for the Sci Fi Channel during the previous year on the subject of the alleged 1965 UFO crash at the Pennsylvanian town of Kecksburg. No one really knew whether or not a UFO, or Russian spy satellite, as some suspected, had crashed at Kecksburg, but filming the show had allowed me to forge new links within the American entertainment world—hence the call.

The man grandly informed me that he was on an important and groundbreaking quest to secure interesting and original tales on the unexplained that could be turned into mini-cinematic masterpieces for *Proof Positive*. Not only that: *Proof Positive* paid hard cash for stories. Struck by this truly extraordinary, and very welcome, revelation, I immediately sat upright, and said that I would obligingly do whatever I could to help him.

And thus was borne a week-long adventure deep in the heart of Puerto Rico's El Yunque rain forest that primarily revolved around dead and decayed chickens, vampire saliva, vomit, or even sperm, depending on whose rumor mill you accept as the truth, and the consumption of voluminous amounts of that most blessed and sacred of all drinks: the frozen margarita, sans salt.

After having listened to him relate to me the format of *Proof Positive*, which ultimately proved to be a fairly well-executed combination of *The X-Files* and *CSI*, and that had, as he explained it, "a scientific and forensic analysis of the evidence in support of each story" as its cornerstone, I did what I often did under such circumstances: I phoned several of my old friends back in England to (a) see if they could help; and (b) get them on board. One of those was none other than Jonathan Downes of the Center for Fortean Zoology. Via a late-night, transatlantic telephone call to Jon, I informed him that the show was looking for quality stories that focused upon what was broadly termed "the unexplained," but that there had to be some sort of relevant, physical evidence that could

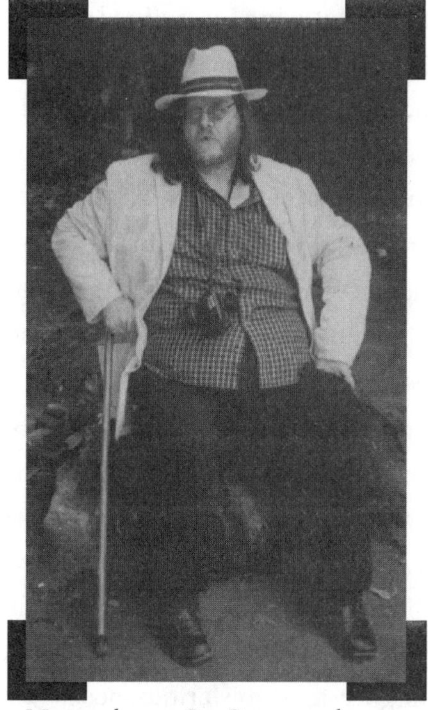

Monster-hunter Jon Downes takes a break in a spooky cave, while he and I search for vampires in Puerto Rico.

be made available for scientific study.

"Can you help?" I asked Jon, who was at the time, quite literally, engaged in carnal activities with his latest flame.

"There's good money involved—four figures worth," I added.

Quick as a flash, Jon had the answer, as I knew he undoubtedly would: "What about a dead chicken that was attacked by a Chupacabras?" he inquired, excitedly, while simultaneously leaving his bed partner. Indeed, he sounded so upbeat about the idea that I could practically see the dollar signs revolving wildly in his eyeballs already.

"A dead chicken? You have a dead chicken from a Chupacabras attack?" I replied, with stark and surreal visions in my mind of the rotting, maggot-infested beast lying sprawled, legs akimbo, on Jon's living room carpet. I had actually seen much worse lying in such a state on the floor of Jon's somewhat sinister abode, so his response wasn't particularly surprising.

"Well, not exactly," Jon explained, with a laugh. "But I do have a load of feathers taken from the body of a chicken that was supposedly attacked by a Chupacabras when I was in Puerto Rico in 1998. How about we give that to *Proof Positive*, with the possibility that maybe the feathers will contain evidence of Chupacabras DNA that can be analyzed?"

He added, almost apologetically: "Even if it's from a Chupacabras, it might actually be Chupacabras puke or even cum, according to what some of the witnesses said."

Instantly, I knew that this was the story. Whether salivated upon, vomited upon, or even screwed by the Chupacabras, this wretched piece of feathered decay was about to earn Jon and me a very welcome sum of cash and an all-expenses-paid, weeklong trip to the blisteringly hot climes of the island of Puerto Rico in search of monsters. But for the uninitiated, a word (or several), about the island's most mighty and mysterious beast, the Chupacabras.

Since at least the mid-1990s, dark and sinister stories have surfaced from the forests and lowlands of Puerto Rico that tell of a strange creature roaming the landscape, while striking overwhelming terror into the hearts of the populace, which is not surprising because the animal was described as having a pair of glowing red eyes, powerful, claw-like hands, razor-sharp teeth, a body not unlike that a monkey, and occasionally large and leathery bat-like wings. And if that were not enough, the beast was feeding on the blood of the local animal population. Puerto Rico had a monstrous vampire in its midst.

Theories abounded, and still do, with some researchers and witnesses suggesting that the beast was some form of giant bat; others preferred the rumor that it had extraterrestrial origins; while the most bizarre idea postulated was that the Chupacabras was the creation of a Top Secret, CIA-controlled genetic research lab that was hidden deep within Puerto Rico's El Yunque rain forest.

On Thursday, July 15, 2004, I flew to Denver, Colorado, where I was scheduled to speak at the annual symposium of the Mutual UFO Network on the subject of a particular type of UFO that has become known as the "Black Triangle," and one that has been seen regularly in the skies of practically every corner of the planet for approximately the last two decades. As the name suggests, these critters are black, incredibly large, triangular-shaped, and quite a lot of people have seen them flying around in the dead of night, while simultaneously also having the proverbial shit scared out of them by the presence of these mysterious craft.

Personally, I suspected that most of them were next-generation *Stealth*-type aircraft piloted by burly United States Air Force pilots. However, that particular theory did not go well with the small fraction of the audience that desperately wanted to hear that the Black Triangles were manned by skinny, little bald guys with big, black eyes and over-sized heads, who originated from, well, take your pick: Zeta Reticuli, Mars, Venus, the Crab Nebula; and so on.

As I knew it inevitably would be, the event was a mind-numbingly sober and spectacularly staid affair, and one that was filled with a lot of serious and scientific discussion and waffle about all matters extraterrestrial and, regrettably, not a great deal else.

And therefore, I retired to the bar whenever possible with like-minded friends, and where the discussion focused upon just about anything and everything *but* UFOs.

The conference was a three-day event, most of which, thanks to the effects of my two closest and forever trustworthy friends, Jack 'n' Coke, was a blur, and therefore it was, but a short time before I was on a return flight to Dallas and back to the comfort of home—but not for long, however. Twenty-four hours later, after Dana and I had the opportunity to test the bedsprings to their absolute limit, I was on my way to Puerto Rico: *Project Dead Chicken* had officially begun.

Having slightly more than liberally imbibed on the flight from Dallas to my connection point at Orlando, Florida, and feeling somewhat evil of mind, I successfully reduced the old lady sitting next to me on the plane to a quivering wreck, after I regaled her with highly exaggerated tale after highly exaggerated tale of the diabolical exploits of the Chupacabras. Truly it was a good day to be alive, I thought to myself, as I carefully watched the horrified woman extract a plentiful supply of pills from a full-to-the-brim bottle, and shakily pop two of them into her heavily wrinkled mouth.

And when she informed me that her final destination was none other than the city of San Juan, Puerto Rico, and that she was now unlikely to get a good night's sleep while she was there, all thanks to me, I knew that my task for the day had been successfully accomplished. I closed my eyes, reclined in my seat, and slept soundly until the bump and slight skid on the runway alerted me to the fact that we had landed at Orlando.

I had barely an hour to make my connection, and so, as I stepped off the aircraft somewhat pickled of brain, I quickly said my goodbyes to my newly found, elderly friend. She merely glared at me in a "screw you" fashion. I would never see the aged woman again; however, I often wonder how she fared during her stay in San Juan, and whether or not the specter of the Chupacabras looming over her, not to mention its deadly, vampire-like activities, had an adverse effect on her time on the island.

The flight to Puerto Rico from Orlando with a local charter company was great fun, and the riotous atmosphere aboard the plane was almost akin to that of an out-of-control party just before being broken up by the cops. Alcohol and heavy rock music were supplied in massive doses, and the stewardesses were all curiously and amusingly referred to over the plane's intercom as "the talent." Bizarre, it was, indeed. But fun, oh yes.

After having arrived at San Juan and having collected my bags, I stepped into the arrival area of what was without a doubt the most densely packed and hottest airport I have ever been in. The combined and unmistakable odors of human sweat, unwashed clothes, and exotic food swamped my nostrils, and I looked around for a handheld sign that I was told would have my name on it. Sure enough, after a few minutes of wandering around the airport, I caught sight of my quarry. I waved, and an attractive woman who I estimated to be in her 20s waved back.

"Hi, I'm Carola," she said, with a smile, as I reached her.

It transpired that Carola, who was the producer, chief researcher, and general organizer of the show that we would ultimately make, both lived and worked on the island of Puerto Rico, and had been hired in a freelance capacity by the Sci Fi Channel. I was greatly impressed by the professionalism of Carola's work as, on the journey to our hotel, she related to me the details of the vast and varied body of witnesses she had located for us to speak with, as well as the many locations that we would be investigating.

It was around 5 p.m. when we arrived at the Wind Chimes Hotel and, after a much-welcomed shower, I headed down to the open air bar for a spectacularly delicious chicken salad made from a wide variety of local delicacies. Carola introduced me to both the director and the cameraman who would accompany Jon and me on our quest to seek out the Chupacabras: David Vassar and Kevin O'Brien, respectively. David was a genial fellow in his 50s with a shock of long, wavy, white hair, and a permanent smile. Kevin, meanwhile, was a skinny and ultra-intense guy with a fantastic flair for ideas and technical wizardry.

As we all got to know each other, and as I was quite literally digesting the last morsel of my culinary delight, I felt a heavy and sweat-soaked hand upon my shoulder. It was, of course, Jon, just arrived after a tiring, daylong flight from England.

"Waiter!" the mighty behemoth bellowed. "Bring me a large margarita on the rocks, and bring it now!"

Bear hugs exchanged, we all sat down together to discuss our course of action. Thankfully, this took practically no time at all, as Carola had every step of the expedition planned almost to the minute. At 8 a.m. the following morning, she explained, we would all meet outside of the hotel, where we would set off in military-convoy-style for our first location: the farm of a chicken breeder whose produce had been the victim of a particularly strange and violent Chupacabras attack.

"Are we traveling with you?" Jon eagerly asked Carola, whose buxom and wholesome form he had taken an immediate and particular liking to.

"Sorry, Jon, no," she replied, smiling. "I've hired you and Nick a cool-looking, silver jeep to drive around in."

Jon and I grinned at each other, devoured our drinks, and toasted the fun that was to come with a fresh round of Margaritas. Shortly afterward, David and Kevin retired to their respective beds, Carola headed to her nearby home, and me and Jon chatted until the early hours of the morning with the hotel barmaid, who had a particular fascination, with what was arguably Puerto Rico's very own equivalent of the Loch Ness Monster, Mothman, and Bigfoot all combined into one. Mind you, the rest of the customers, who were doing their collective best, but failing, to pretend that they were not listening to our strange exchanges on monster hunting, thought that we were completely and utterly mad. Perhaps we were. But we didn't care. We hung out until closing time and then stumbled to our rooms for some well-earned sleep.

At 7 a.m. the following morning, my alarm sounded. I showered, then headed down to the breakfast bar, where I met Jon, who was having a particularly difficult time walking due to a violent attack of hemorrhoids that had hit him with spectacular speed and ferocity during the previous week.

"They're hanging like a bunch of bloody grapes," he complained loudly, as we ate a breakfast of fruit and coffee. "And it's not funny either, Nicholas," he added, after I commented that perhaps the unfortunate timing of his attack was due to the diabolical work of a covert arm of the "secret government," which had targeted him with a particularly virulent form of biological warfare, in an attempt to prevent us from uncovering the truth about the Chupacabras.

Five minutes later, David and Kevin joined us, and shortly afterward, a screech of brakes outside indicated that Carola and the rest of the film crew had arrived. We stepped out into the already-blistering morning heat to see our jeep, its silver paint shining brightly under the Puerto Rican sun. As I was the one with an American driver's license, Jon would become the passenger and I would be the chauffeur. David and Kevin headed off with Carola, we followed, and the film crew, which was led by a genial fellow with the curious nickname of "Cheese," fell in behind us in two trucks packed to the brim with camera gear, audio equipment, and more. Already wired for sound, we headed for the farm of a man named Noel, and our first encounter with the work of the Chupacabras.

The view en route was both amazing and infinitely varied: The lush greenery of the El Yunque rain forest dominated the skyline, open-air restaurants serving all manner of culinary delights peppered the highway, small children played in the gutters, menacing packs of dogs roamed the roads in a fashion akin to that of a 1950s New York street gang, and homes that ranged from pitifully weather-beaten shacks to large, impressive-looking villas were staple parts of the environment.

Until a person actually spends time traveling the island and personally speaks with witnesses, government employees, police officers, and ranchers (all of whom have been implicated in the mystery to varying degrees) as will become apparent, it is incredibly difficult to appreciate precisely how much the Chupacabras mystery has become ingrained in Puerto Rican society. But we were about to find out.

Noel was a chicken breeder; however, he did not raise poultry for food. Rather, he lovingly and carefully reared the beasts specifically so that they could be used in cock-fighting tournaments in the small arena that was situated on his property. Neither Jon nor I were fans of blood sports, but we had to remember, that this was not our country or culture, and it was certainly not our place to tell people on the other side of the world how to live their lives just because we happened to disagree with their ways and customs.

But back to Noel and his curious encounter with the unknown. Greetings exchanged, with cameras and audio equipment set up, and with Carola translating for us, we roamed around Noel's small farm as he relayed to Jon and me a tale of genuinely spooky proportions. Some months previously, he had awakened during the hours of darkness on one particular morning to the sound of his chickens literally screaming down the house. Much to his chagrin, however, Noel failed to get out of bed, and waited until dawn broke to see what all the fuss had been about. He told us that he was horrified to find all of his prized birds dead. Not only were they dead: they had two small puncture wounds on their necks, and their bodies had been drained of blood.

"We need a cross, some garlic, and a wooden stake, mate," Jon whispered to me, with a look of genuine concern on his face, as Noel pointed to the cages where the chickens had been held. But what made this particular case so intriguing and memorable was the fact that whatever had killed the chickens had first carefully and quietly opened the complex locks on each of the cages before evacuating them of blood. This suggested that a diabolically sophisticated degree of cunning, intelligence, and dexterity was at work.

Noel demonstrated how genuinely difficult it was to undo the locks, and openly admitted how baffled, concerned, and even scared he had been in the aftermath of the carnage. He had no doubt that the killings represented the presence of something truly evil in his midst. We all agreed. Indeed, even David and Kevin were impressed by Noel's sincerity and his description of what had occurred. An hour or so later, and after repeated filming of Jon and I interviewing Noel, we departed and headed for our next location: a complex series of deep caves on the island that were rumored to be the lair of the beast. Jon and I climbed into the jeep and followed the rest of the team along the highway to the site in question, merrily singing along to the joyful and ear-splitting tunes of Sham 69—a British punk-rock band of the late 1970s, whose CD of greatest hits I had brought along for the journey.

After stopping for lunch at what was really little more than a hut, but where the local cuisine, ice-cold beer, and service were all first class, we were ready to tackle the caves. Clambering around dark and dank caverns and tunnels provided me with a distinct and curious sense of déjà vu. Before leaving England in 2001, I had searched a series of caves and tunnels, beneath the county of Wiltshire, that were the property of the Royal Air Force, where it was rumored that a species of giant worm made its lair. I never actually found the worm, however, it was certainly odd that after that excursion, here I was, three years later, roaming around similarly darkened caves on the other side of the world; but this time I was in search of monstrous vampires, assisted by a fellow who went by the name of Cheese. Sane, life was not.

Interestingly, throughout the cave system, vampire bats could be seen and heard soaring and circling above us. Occasionally we would catch sight of their piercing eyes when our flashlights illuminated their evil-looking visages. In fact, both Jon and I seriously considered the possibility that the Chupacabras was a type of vampire bat, albeit a large one: a *very* large one. That would, we thought, explain the occasionally reported large and leathery wings, the creature's somewhat monkey-like face, and its particular penchant for fresh blood. Were there *really* man-sized bats haunting the rain forests of Puerto Rico? It was as good a theory as any other, we thought; and, to an extent, I still do.

We roamed around the caves for hours as David and Kevin had us discuss for the camera what it was that we were doing, and how, by delving deep into the heart of the cavernous maze, we might actually stand a chance of uncovering the beast's underground lair. David insisted that I wear a black t-shirt, black sunglasses, and cargo pants for the entire escapade, which I was very happy with: I have a large collection of black t-shirts that I like wear at every possible opportunity. He suggested Jon attire himself as a 21st century equivalent of Sherlock Holmes-meets-Indiana Jones, which he did in splendid style, and with a high degree of flair and panache. In fact, so pleased were David and Kevin by what they considered to be highly amusing visual imagery, they both expressed the firm opinion that the two of us should undertake *all* of the investigations for *Proof Positive*. Despite their, and our, enthusiasm, sadly, it was not to be.

As with our experience in the tunnels under the British countryside, our search of Puerto Rico's underground did not succeed in disgorging the Chupacabras. But it did reap some pretty good film footage of me scrambling through this underground labyrinth with flashlight in hand, while Jon complained loudly that none of this activity was good for his diabetes, his strained back, or his hemorrhoids.

Essentially, that was the first day of filming. We then headed for the comfort of the Wind Chimes Hotel and a night of partying. And although Jon and I were used to operating in a distinctly odd and twilight world where nothing was quite as it seemed, even we were surprised by the revelations that would surface later that night. We met at the bar around 7 p.m. and ordered drinks and dinner, which for Jon was a delicious-looking concoction of Puerto Rican cuisine that the barmaid had recommended, and which, for me, was a well-cooked steak. We chatted about the day's events and congratulated each other on the fact that, at the considerable cost of the Sci Fi Channel, we were having an uproarious, all-expenses-paid romp around Puerto Rico chasing distinctly strange beasts.

And then things got a bit weird. Or perhaps weirder would be a better description.

Kevin joined us and we got to know this quiet character a lot better. It transpired that as a freelance cameraman, Kevin lived a fascinating life, and he regaled us with accounts of his time filming in the Himalayas and other spectacular locations around the world. But it was his monster-hunting excursions that really grabbed our attention. Several years prior, Kevin had been involved in the filming of a television documentary on the famous lake monster dubbed Ogopogo, the Nessie-like inhabitant of Okanagan Lake, British Columbia, Canada. Kevin told us that he had spent a lengthy period of time at the lake with a film crew, documenting sightings of the long-necked beast, and had secured many a good interview with witnesses to the activities of whatever it was that really lurked within the darkened waters of the lake.

"So, did you actually see Ogopogo?" I asked, fully expecting a response in the negative.

"Well," Kevin said, thoughtfully, "we didn't see Ogopogo, but early one morning there was a sighting of a large snake that crossed the road toward the lake."

"How big was it?" I inquired, with my curiosity well and truly piqued.

"Oh, about 30 to 40 feet, I would say," replied Kevin, matter-of-factly.

Jon and I looked at each other incredulously.

"Kevin, my dear boy," Jon said. "You do know that snakes of that length don't exist anywhere in North America or Canada, don't you?"

"No, I didn't," he replied, in equally matter-of-fact fashion.

"That was Ogopogo!" exclaimed Jon, adding: "Didn't it occur to you that if someone saw a 40-foot-long snake-like creature crossing the road near a lake that supposedly is home to a snake-like monster, that you really *did* see the Ogopogo?"

"Oh yeah," said Kevin, with a look of sudden realization on his face. "I hadn't thought of it like that." And the weirdness continued.

Shortly afterward, an American couple sat down at the other end of the 20-foot-long bar and, upon overhearing snippets of our conversation and learning from the Chupacabras-obsessed barmaid that we were there to make a show about the island's most famous monster, they informed us that while camping in an area of Washington State forest a number of years before, they had had a brief encounter with a large, lumbering beast of the type that most of us know best as Bigfoot.

Admittedly, there was little for the couple to tell us beyond the fact that it was late at night when they heard strange, heavy breathing outside of their tent that was accompanied by an overpowering and gut-churning stench. On crawling out, they were startled to see for a brief moment a large, hairy, man-like figure standing in the darkness that headed off at a high speed into the dense cover of the thick trees after it realized the terrified couple was staring directly at it.

"This is getting bloody ridiculous!" Jon shouted, while simultaneously raising his arms into the air in an exasperated fashion. "We're in Puerto Rico chasing vampires and on one side of us we've got a cameraman telling us about Ogopogo, and on the other side we've got a couple who saw Bigfoot. This is all too bloody surreal." I couldn't argue with Jon on that point at all. But madness and the world of the surreal and the synchronistic were part and parcel of our everyday lives. So we simply catalogued the data and ordered a fresh round of margaritas, a piece of strawberry cheesecake, and discussed what Carola had told us the next day would bring: an interview with a lady named Norka who had seen a Chupacabras up close and personal in the mid-1970s.

Norka was an elderly lady who lived in a truly beautiful home high in the El Yunque rain forest, which one could only reach by successfully negotiating an infinitely complex series of treacherous roads that had been built perilously close to the edge of some very steep hills, and that, on more than one occasion, we came very close to toppling over. "It's a good job we have you in the jeep, Jon, to keep the weight balanced," I quipped, as we hurtled violently around the hilltops. Jon merely shot me a worried look, peered out of the passenger window into the darkened depths of the valley below, and said nothing.

The Caribbean National Forest, as El Yunque is known, was a glorious sight to behold. Around 28,000 acres in size, and located in the rugged Sierra de Luquillo, which is approximately 25 miles southeast of the city of San Juan, it was named after the benevolent Indian spirit, Yuquiyu, and is the only rain forest in the U.S. National Forest System. I learned from a forest guide in the area that more than 100 billion gallons of precipitation fall each year, creating the jungle-like ambience of lush foliage, sparkling leaves, spectacular waterfalls, shining wet rocks, and shadowy paths that really have to be seen up close and personal to be appreciated. The Forest contains rare wildlife, too, including the Puerto Rican parrot, the Puerto Rican boa snake, a multitude of lizards, and crabs, and the famous coqui frog, so named after its strange and unique vocalizations.

Traveling in convoy, it was mid-afternoon when we finally arrived, and, the perfect host, Norka welcomed us with open arms, fed us, refreshed our dehydrated bodies, and gave us a guided tour of her home. Evidently, word had got around that Norka was due to be interviewed, so the road outside of her home was full of people, all eager to see what was going to take place.

As the crew set up their equipment, and Jon fumbled with his camcorder, Norka told me how she was one of the first women on the island to own a motorbike, and she showed me numerous, old, black-and-white photographs of her as a young girl, perched proudly on her sturdy hog. She was also a gifted artist, and I was truly honored when she presented me with a glorious color rendition of the Chupacabras that she had seen all those years before. Norka's life was a rich and fascinating one in every sense, and I was pleased for her. And then it was time for the filming to begin in earnest.

Although the exact date escaped her, Norka told us that she was driving home one night in 1975 or 1976, when she was both startled and horrified by the shocking sight of a bizarre creature shambling across the road. She described the animal as being approximately 4 feet in height, and having a monkey-like body that was covered in dark brown hair or fur, wings that were a cross between those of a bat and a bird, and glowing eyes that bulged alarmingly from a bat-style visage. Elongated fingers, with sharp, claw-like appendages, which looked like they could inflict serious damage, flicked ominously in Norka's direction. She could only sit and stare as the beast then turned its back on her and rose slowly into the sky.

Everyone was pleased with Norka's account: It was without a doubt one of the most credible that we came across during our time on the island. But it was time to go and meet a man named Ishmael, who was going to tell us all about a bunch of dead peacocks. But before we went off in search of the man who told us to call him Ishmael, Jon and I sat on the hood of the jeep, musing upon something that was curiously intriguing.

By her own admission, Norka was unsure if her encounter had occurred in 1975 or 1976. If it was the latter date then it was highly significant, because it was in that year that a creature, which looked surprisingly similar to one displayed in Norka's painting, began to be seen within a sleepy area of England known as Mawnan Woods—home to an old church and an ancient Earthwork constructed way back in prehistoric times. On various occasions in 1976, numerous witnesses, who were usually young girls, saw a diabolical creature lurking within the woods that became known as the Owlman.

There was little doubt that the Owlman was, like so many other strange creatures, paranormal in origin and diabolically evil in nature. It had a large body that was half-man, half-bird, a huge pair of wings, and devilishly glowing red eyes. Plus, the area around the old Church was saturated in Witchcraft (in times both past and present), and an oppressive atmosphere seemed to dominate the black heart of Mawnan woods. Jon had dug into the story of the Owlman for years, and his intensely personal investigation to resolve the mystery had literally taken him to the brink of madness. Today, Jon refuses to discuss his times chasing the creature, ever fearful that the psychic backlash that plagued and tormented him for years might return and forever pursue him—similar to an obsessed Captain Ahab seeking out the great white whale, Moby Dick. Jon and I continued to sit on the hood for a while, wondering to ourselves, quite seriously, if the Owlman had cunningly steered us toward Norka in an attempt to, once again, get its claws into Jon's tortured mind. Jon tried to banish the thought from his mind and we continued on with the next task in hand.

Ishmael proved to be a very interesting guy, who had the enviable task of being an official investigator of the Chupacabras for Puerto Rico's Civil Defense Department, and who had collected a veritable mountain of material and testimony on the beast. He had no doubt that some form of unknown, utterly lethal killing machine was indeed lurking deep within the darker corners of the island. To illustrate this, Ishmael directed us to a farm high in the hills where the owner had lost an entire collection of peacocks to the diabolical predator. As the crew filmed, again a familiar story was told to us of animals drained of blood, of vampire-style puncture wounds on the necks of the birds, and of an overwhelming paranoid fear that would pervade the entire area after darkness fell.

We spent three more days in Puerto Rico. Time and again we heard eerily similar and chilling accounts, and spent a wealth of time recreating for the cameras Jon's experience of several years prior, when he had succeeded in extracting DNA samples from the body of the unfortunate chicken that was responsible for our strange and current activities. And although *Proof Positive's* forensic team did not ultimately find any other, unknown DNA on the chicken feathers that Jon provided to them, by the end of the week, I would not have been surprised had we bumped into a cape-wearing vampire, of the classic Hollywood style, parading around Old San Juan, such was the credibility of the tales of blood-sucking carnage told to us. We could have stayed a week longer and still not even touched on 1 percent of all the cases that had surfaced over the course of the last decade. But time was not on our side—and neither was the Sci Fi Channel's budget.

And so, after a final night of festivities, in which we all toasted to new friendships and a job well done, I went for a midnight stroll around Old San Juan. It was a magical couple of hours and not unlike a trip back in time to an era long gone. I wandered the small, cobbled streets and the darkened alleys (which, with hindsight, was probably not a good idea at 1 a.m. on a Sunday morning), taking in the smell of exotic, cooked food, stale beer, and the laughs and chatter of the crowds out for a night's entertainment in the little inns and bars that dominated the area. Streetlights flickered and dogs barked as I wandered a part of the city that appeared not to have changed since the days of the pirates. Looking out at the harsh sea that was lit up by the fullest of moons, I half expected to see a creaking ghost ship, with its skull and crossbones flag flying menacingly as the waves crashed against its wooden frame. The lack of Blackbeard, Bluebeard, and the rest of their motley ilk was easily compensated by what I did see, however.

There was La Muralla—the old city wall, the bulk of which was built between 1539 and 1641 out of 20-foot-thick sandstone blocks, and that protected the city against enemy attacks. At the western mouth of the bay I could see Isla de Cabras (or Goat Island, to give it its English translation), and a small Spanish fort, that, I learned from one of the locals, had been built way back in 1610. I then took a stroll to Casa Rosada, or the Pink House. Constructed nearly two centuries previously for the Spanish Army, it had been converted into a daycare center for the children of government workers.

I walked along Recinto Oeste Street and climbed the hill to Plazuela de la Rogativa, a small plaza dominated by a bronze sculpture that recreated the day a bishop and his companions fought with—incredibly, nothing more than torches and chanting—marauding British troops during a 1797 attack on the city. El Morro Fortress was my next stop: A huge military fortification that rose an impressive 140 feet above the sea, was surrounded by the Atlantic Ocean and San Juan Bay. Built between 1540 and 1783 to protect San Juan from attack by sea, El Morro was a veritable maze of secret tunnels and dungeons. Sadly, however, at that time of night, penetrating this magical labyrinth proved impossible. Paseo La

Princesa was a glorious promenade lined with trees, sculptures, and benches, and led to a magnificent fountain that depicted and celebrated Puerto Rico's many and diverse cultural roots. Midway through the promenade was La Princesa itself, a former jail and now, ironically, the headquarters of the Puerto Rico Tourism Company. My last stop was the red-painted Puerta de San Juan, or San Juan Gate, which was one of the six original, and massive, wooden doors that centuries ago were closed at sundown to protect the residents from attack.

Having taken in Old San Juan's impressive history, I headed back to the hotel and packed my bags, ready for the early-morning flight back to Dallas. Just before I climbed into bed, I took one last look at the breathtaking sight of the city lights, the lush, green hills, and the ocean. I breathed deeply, exhaled, and smiled to myself. Truly the life of a monster hunter was a good one.

Ironically, one of the most notable accounts that I uncovered on the Chupacabras mystery came not during our shoot with the *Proof Positive* team, but a week later, in a lengthy phone conversation after returned to Dallas. I spoke with a lady named Rosa who had a remarkable tale to tell. It was 1991 and Rosa, who worked in a small restaurant on the island, was driving home with a friend after a Friday night out in Old San Juan. For a reason that to this day she is unable to determine, both Rosa and her friend felt compelled to drive their car high into the El Yunque rain forest, something, she told me, she would never have normally done, and certainly not on a Saturday morning.

Nevertheless, the pair duly headed along the snaking roads that lead up to the forest, and, subsequently, were confronted by a horrific sight while rounding one particular bend: a 4- to 5-foot-tall animal that crossed the road in front of them at a distance of about 50 to 60 feet with an awkward, shuffling gait. The creature appeared to be very dark gray in color, and had two large wings that seemed to be wrapped around its back, giving the appearance of a long cloak that dragged on the surface of the road as it walked.

Rosa and her friend were terrified, and watched in horror as the beast continued to slowly cross the road. The creature glared at them for a split second with a pair of what Rosa determined were self-illuminating, glowing red eyes. Too shocked to do anything but stare in awe, the pair continued to watch as the animal shuffled into the trees and bushes and was lost from sight.

Thirteen years after her experience, Rosa spoke in a nervous voice as she related her account to me. Other than her family and several close friends (including a friend of one of the interviewees encountered during our visit to Puerto Rico, who had arranged the interview with Rosa for me), Rosa had discussed the encounter with no one. For her, the most bizarre aspect of the encounter was not the sighting itself, but the fact that the creature somehow compelled her—she believes—to drive to the El Yunque rain forest with the express intention of ensuring that she saw it, and for purposes that neither she nor I can adequately determine. If nothing else, Rosa's account demonstrated to me that the mystery of the Chupacabras was a truly strange and very real one, and it showed no signs of stopping.

In early December 2004, ironically at the time that the Chupacabras episode of *Proof Positive* aired in the United States, no fewer than 11 goats were found slaughtered inside their wooden pen at the Illusion children's park in Rio Piedras, Puerto Rico. The discovery had been made by the owner of the park's petting zoo, Fausto Radaelli, who had taken the goats to the park the previous Monday with the intention of recreating "a manger scene for the Christmas holiday." Two days, later, however, the animals were dead.

A December 3, 2004, article in the *Primera Hora* newspaper stated: "Three of the goats presented large bite marks, dismemberment, and one of them had half of its body devoured; all of its internal organs, excepting its stomach, were gone. The rest of the goats had bite marks and fang marks on the rear of their bodies. The marks resembled the ones found on animals allegedly attacked by the infamous Chupacabras."

However, Ernesto Marquez, a biologist and a specialist in exotic animals, concluded that the goats were attacked by "a wolf, a coyote, a hybrid, or very large feral dogs." Marquez continued: "These are regular fang marks. Canids kill animals by the rear, seizing them to hold them down and eat them. The animal leaped; it is an agile animal, attacking from the rear. It's astute and knows human beings. This is vicious. The animal isn't psychologically well."

The site was also examined by Julio Diaz, of the Animal Control Solutions Company, as well as by veterinary technician Herman Sulsona of the San Juan Animal Control Center. Although Marquez was convinced that the killings had a down-to-earth explanation, there were no signs of forcible entry in the animals' pen. More intriguing: No prints or hairs were found of any other animal aside from the goats themselves. The mystery—perhaps inevitably—remained precisely that: a mystery.

Only days after this event occurred, I had the opportunity to speak with the director of a new movie that was being made on the Chupacabras. And as with the real-life exploits of the beast, the events that led to the making of the movie seemed to have more than an air of both the paranormal and the synchronistic about them. Titled *Cabras*, the movie was the first in a trilogy of productions on the Chupacabras planned by Polania Pictures.

Thanks to the assistant producer, Monica Polania, I was able to conduct an exclusive interview with the director, producer, cinematographer, and editor of *Cabras*, Fredy Polania, who advised me that: "If I were to classify the movie in a short description, I would say that it is *The Exorcist* meets *The Texas Chain Saw Massacre*." This was fine with me as I practically lived on a diet of intense, ultra-violent, zombie-horror-slasher movies.

Polania added: "I was born of Colombian parents who resided in Napa, California, for 18 years, and the world of cinema has inspired me ever since I was a child. And I guess what really got me involved in filmmaking was the director Francis Ford Coppola, who also lives in Napa. His way of making movies really taught me a true sense of what I call guerilla filmmaking."

And what was it that prompted Polania to cross paths with Puerto Rico's notoriously ferocious beast? I wanted to know.

Polania explained: "The unknown has always intrigued me. The mysteries behind such things as crop circles, spirits, and paranormal activities led me to look at the Chupacabras. There are so many questions: Is it a beast? Is it a demon? Does it have an alien source? Or is it possibly the devil himself? And how can one entity cause so much havoc, and never get captured?"

This last question posed by Polania was a very good one, and reinforced my own, personal theories that the Chupacabras, similar to many of the other mysterious creatures that allegedly populate our planet, such as Bigfoot, the Yeti, and a wide variety of lake monsters, were thought-forms-come-to-life, and had Tulpa-like origins, rather than being conventional, physical creatures. Indeed, this was further borne out by the fact that, when the episode of *Proof Positive* that chronicled our Puerto Rican adventures aired in December 2004, the only thing that the forensic team could find on the remains of the dastardly chicken was DNA from the animal itself. Whatever had caused all of the carnage had left no tell-tale calling card, again reinforcing for me, at least, the notion that the Chupacabras had its origins in the world of the paranormal.

Meanwhile, back to Polania, who expanded further: "For the past 15 years, the mutilations and the deaths have terrorized us. And so our story begins."

"Let me ask you this," he said to me, "when you stare in a dark room and you see things, you ask yourself, 'Is it really there?' And to most people, the mystery behind the Chupacabras is in their minds. But the proof is here. The animal mutilations alone are proof—to me—that this is something extraterrestrial. Personally, I believe it's real. I think it's waiting to reveal itself. But why it hasn't already, I don't know. But there is something out there far beyond what we can even imagine."

Polania continued: "My belief is that the Chupacabras is extraterrestrial; but I also believe that there is something much higher to this—maybe spiritual, maybe biblical, even. And it is said that at the end of time, a beast would walk the Earth."

Intriguing words, I thought to myself. And Polania had equally intriguing comments and observations to make concerning the way in which the cast and crew of *Cabras* came together on the movie:

"Before a single shot was ever captured, I had put together a crew; but not by the usual way of placing ads in newspapers. It had to be something much more special, so I put together the crew through my own intuition. And what we found was that the movie started to manifest itself. I call my crew my research team, as they are something much more than just a crew. Beginning in the summer of 2000, we traveled to different parts of the world and took eyewitness accounts and collected stories from people. What we found shocked us. I can tell you that the world has been going about this the wrong way. If people knew what was really going on out there, they would not treat the Chupacabras as a joke."

In a similar vein, Polania stated to me: "The cast feel like they've done this already and it's almost as if we've all met before and as if we were brought together by fate. It was almost as if we were brought together by something greater."

I asked Polania how he thought the movie would be viewed and interpreted by those with an interest in the mystery of the

Chupacabras, as well as by the general public and the media. Would it be perceived as just another horror movie? Polania was unequivocal in his views:

"I think this movie is going to be an eye-opener. I want to stress that *Cabras* is not a movie about death. It's a movie about something that lives among us. I think that with our movie the public will find a new perspective on what the paranormal is really about."

On the subject of Polania Pictures, he explained to me that: "Our crew is quite small. Our philosophy is that you don't need a million dollars to make a great film. The company is based on the trust of friends and it is the love of movies that brought us all together. We all dedicated four years of our lives with no pay to make this movie. The movie could never have been done without the closeness and trust we had in each other. *Cabras* is the first film from this group of friends and family."

Fredy Polania stated to me in closing: "This is something I was born to do. The unknown and the mystery of it is something I have to tell. And what better way than in a movie?"

What better way, indeed? I could only conclude, based on my and Jon's adventures on Puerto Rico, the inhabitants of the island whom we spoke with, and my interview with Fredy Polania, that both off-screen and on-screen, the exploits of the diabolical and monstrous Chupacabras were destined to continue.

10

On the Track of Bigfoot

From mid-to-late 2004, I found myself thrust deep in the heart of the Bigfoot controversy. It all began in May of that year, when an envelope arrived in my mailbox with an Oregon-based postmark. This was one of a number of items in the box, and I attached no particular significance to it. What a mistake that was. When I finally got around to opening the letter and reading it the following day, I was, to say the least, startled by its contents. It came from a lady, now in late-middle age, living in a particular town in the aforementioned state of Oregon, and who worked as an events-organizer for a perfume company. She had recently read my book, *Three Men Seeking Monsters,* and was looking for someone to speak with about "some photographs" that she had acquired after the recent death of her father that "will amaze you and that show a Bigfoot."

She supplied a phone number and asked if I would call her, which I duly did. People often contact me making extreme claims, but with little evidence to back up their assertions. I telephoned with no particular expectation of anything, but this call turned out not to be your average, everyday conversation at all. After we exchanged greetings, the woman informed me that her father had been a senior figure in American politics in Washington State in the 1950s and was also an avid hunter.

To summarize the conversation: Her father had been out hunting alone on a Sunday morning in the summer of 1952, in a certain area of dense forest land in northern Washington State. He had been stalking deer for several hours and was sitting in a clearing, drinking from a container of water when his attention was firmly captured by the shocking sight of a large, hair-covered creature roaming through a thinly wooded area near to where her father was taking a rest from the day's activities. He continued to watch as the creature lumbered through the trees, pounding on several trunks as it did so.

"Dad said it almost amused him, as if the animal was angry at something and was hitting the tree trunks in anger," the woman told me. She speculated that the creature's actions distracted its attention from her father because when only about 30 feet from him, it suddenly stopped in its tracks and stared right at him with what seemed like a monumental look of surprise upon its face, and its jaw dropped slightly but noticeably.

The creature, her father stated, was immense, possibly 8 feet in height, *very* muscular, with long, powerful arms, and a wide head that sat square on its shoulders atop a barely noticeable neck. The animal was covered in shiny black hair that seemed to cover all of its body apart from its face. And although it was human-like in shape, the man was of the opinion that it was more animal than human. It then backed away slowly from him, keeping him in view at all times before being lost within the dense trees.

This would have been just another Bigfoot story of the type that I have received on many occasions—except for one thing. The woman claimed to me that she had in her possession a lengthy journal that her father kept at the time, which described the experience in a very detailed fashion, and also three black-and-white photographs that her father took of the animal before it disappeared, and that he developed himself.

"One is very clear and shows it just standing looking at him—he always had his camera," she told me. "Dad said he never knew how he was able to not shake while he took the pictures, but he did it, I think, without thinking; just grabbed his camera and took the pictures. If he had stopped to think, he probably wouldn't do it. The picture is very clear: you see all the body down to the knees and the head and eyes but with a lot of shadows for the rest."

The two remaining pictures, she added, showed the animal as it was in the process of backing away out of sight. Interestingly, she advised me that she had had a keen, but private, interest in Bigfoot for many years because of her father's encounter, and made a lot of comments about Bigfoot lore. Notably, she considered the famous film footage of Bigfoot taken in 1967 by Bigfoot hunter Roger Patterson to be bogus for one key reason: "The animal my dad photographed has long, ape-like arms. It looks very like a very large animal and less like a man. But that film: the arms look human in length. That made me suspicious." Naturally, I asked for verification and confirmation of the story, and duly received copies of photographs of her father taken during the course of his employment at official functions, including one with a well-known figure in 1950s American politics, and various official records that confirm his position.

The Bigfoot photographs and the journal were frustratingly—some might say, inevitably—elusive, however, and remained so, largely due to the woman's concerns about how this would ultimately play out and specifically with respect to her father's reputation, which was, perhaps, understandable.

Of course, I knew perfectly well that this could have been nothing more than a hoax, and the woman's claim of being in possession of Bigfoot photographs might even have been the cryptozoological equivalent of an unverifiable claim to know the name of the second gunman on the Grassy Knoll, or the location of the "alien bodies" from the Roswell UFO crash. And yet, I didn't think so; there were the photographs already received of her father and, more importantly, one photograph of the woman taken with him in 1993, and one taken with him in 1955 (three years after his alleged Bigfoot experience). There was no doubt that these pictures showed the same people, that the man *was* her father, and that he *did* hold a senior position in 1950s Washington State politics.

Through time, the woman contacted me less and less to the point where, eventually, she refused to take my phone calls. No doubt she had her reasons, and no doubt they were legitimate ones; and, I concluded, they were almost certainly related to her fears for her father's reputation. But perhaps one day, those aged pictures will surface, and at least some of the questions pertaining to the Bigfoot mystery will be firmly laid to rest.

Almost 12 months after Jon Downes and I spent a day with Chester Moore seeking out Bigfoot-like critters in the Deep South of Texas, I, once again, found myself immersed in the mystery of the Lone Star State's most famous man-beast. This time the location was Jefferson, a small town in North Texas that had the reputation of being one of the state's most haunted locations, as I would learn in early 2005 when my path crossed with Vegas magicians Penn & Teller; and, once again, *Proof Positive* researcher, Josh Kessler. But I'm getting ahead of myself here.

Midway through 2003, I met Craig Woolheater, a dedicated researcher of the Bigfoot mystery who lived only a stone's throw from us in the city of Dallas, and who runs the Texas Bigfoot Research Center. "Several of our members have seen these creatures, and that's a big part of the reason we're so passionate about studying them. It's one thing to read about them, but another to see them," said Craig, who had his own encounter with the mystery critter in the early 1990s. It was late one night when Craig and his wife were driving through Louisiana when, out of nowhere: "This big, grayish, hairy creature was on the side of the road. It was dark, but we got a good look at it. The beast was kind of slumped over." And things were never quite the same again for Craig.

"Would you be interested in speaking at our 2004 conference on the subject of the British Bigfoot?" he asked me in June of that year.

"Of course I would," I naturally told him. And it was then that the strangeness began. Craig phoned me a month or so before the conference to tell me that he had booked all of the speakers into a bed-and-breakfast place in Jefferson that was run by a woman named Jeannie Tatum.

"I'll send you details of how to get to Jeannie's place," said Craig.

"You don't need to," I replied.

"Why not?" he asked, somewhat perplexed.

"Jeannie is my wife's aunt," I said, matter-of-factly.

There was a stunned silence for a moment, then: "You're kidding?"

"Nope," I returned. The fact that of all the bed-and-breakfast places in Texas that Craig could have booked his speakers into, he chose upon one run by a member of my own, State-side family was truly bizarre in the extreme. However, it was repeated synchronicities like this that forever plagued numerous colleagues and me whenever we delved into the world of the unknown.

Momentarily flummoxed by this odd situation, Craig regained his thoughts, and I received an official invite to speak at the event, and an eye-opening and memorable experience it was. Dana does not get the opportunity to spend much time with Jeannie, and so it was a good excuse for her to come along, too. She could have cared less about the big, hairy fellow, however.

And so around lunchtime on Friday, October 22, 2004, we headed up to Jefferson from Dallas. That evening, Craig and his colleagues arranged a superb meal for us all at a local outlet, as well as a night of entertaining after-dinner observations from the collective speakers, which included John Kirk III, a fellow Brit also transplanted across the Atlantic. But in John's case, he inhabits Canada, where he is president of the British Columbia Scientific Cryptozoology Club, and the author of the award-winning book, *In The Domain of the Lake Monsters*; Jimmy Chilcutt, latent fingerprint examiner for the Conroe, Texas Police Department, who has undertaken intriguing forensic research into alleged Bigfoot tracks; Rick Knoll, a researcher who has been investigating Bigfoot in a private capacity since 1969; Alton Higgins, a biology professor from Mid-America Christian University in Oklahoma City; Sue Lindley, who discussed her very own Bigfoot sightings in Washington, California, and Oregon; M.K. Davis, who revealed his latest findings and analyses of the film footage taken in 1967 by Roger Patterson that purports to show a Bigfoot; Lee Murphy, author of the crypto-novels *Where Legends Roam* and *Naitaka* (the latter on the subject of legendary lake monster, Ogopogo); and Chester Moore, who was a late addition, and who delivered a great lecture that revealed the sheer scale of his knowledge of the Texan Bigfoot, as well as details of his first-hand investigations in the field.

Early on the Saturday morning, and long before most of the speakers had surfaced, I took a walk around Jeannie's impressively large yard and ran into one of the speakers (who will remain nameless), who was also out taking a stroll. We chatted about our respective research for a while and then returned to the bed-and-breakfast. The door, however, had apparently locked behind me when I had exited it 10 minutes previously, and he and I were stuck outside while everyone else blissfully dreamed of Bigfoot—or whatever it is that cryptozoologists generally dream of.

The speaker had an idea: He pulled out his wallet and extracted a credit card. Just like in a scene from a detective movie, he slipped the card into the lock and tried to force open the door. The Hollywood imagery was soon destroyed, however: The door wouldn't budge, and we were ultimately left to bang on its wooden frame until someone finally heard us. It was certainly surreal in the extreme to be standing outside of a Texas bed-and-breakfast at 6 a.m. on a Saturday morning, with a man who was trying to break into the aforementioned property with a credit card, so that we could retrieve a bunch of plaster casts of Bigfoot tracks.

No harm was done, however, and shortly thereafter, we all headed for the venue, which held an impressive audience in excess of 300. Also, there was Scott Herriott, the one speaker at the event whom I have saved until last. Scott was a stand-up comedian for 11 years and worked at Tech TV for three-and-a-half years as host of *Internet Tonight*. At the Friday night dinner that preceded the conference, Scott revealed that he had grave doubts about the authenticity of the Patterson Film of 1967, but he had no doubt that something was indeed lurking within the deep forests of the Pacific Northwest.

Scott did not limit his experience with Bigfoot to simply talking about the creature and informing the faithful of his theories, however. He went a step further and produced two DVDs on the subject of Bigfoot-hunting, namely: *Journey Toward Squatchdom* and *Squatching*. At the conference, Scott mercilessly promoted and negotiated the sale of his wares to eager buyers of all things Bigfoot-based. And I can state firmly and accurately that he did so in such a fine fashion that he would have had no problem in becoming a prime candidate for a starring role on Donald Trump's *The Apprentice*.

Both of Scott's DVDs were monumentally funny and entertaining, but not in a cruel sense. Essentially, they saw Scott and a variety of buddies, work colleagues, and family members running around forests, drinking beer, visiting the locations of alleged Bigfoot encounters, and having an uproarious good time in the process, but always uncovering some genuinely intriguing data, meeting credible eyewitnesses, and securing friend-of-a-friend-style reports from both down-to-earth characters, and the occasional and inevitable genial oddball.

My own personal experience was that many investigators of unsolved mysteries such as Bigfoot are openly hostile toward anything that, even in an affectionate way, pokes fun at their subject. Similarly, having been involved in the UFO research community for many years, I can safely say that there are a lot of great people within that field, too. But, my God, there are some truly humorless characters out there, also."

But for those such as myself that enjoy being entertained at the same time as actually learning something of value of a cryptozoological nature, I concluded that Scott's produce was the perfect place to start. Both of the productions had a fun, "road-trip" feel to them, and Scott had a dry and cutting sense of humor. Try to imagine a comedic episode of *The X-Files* intertwined with a slightly less intense version of *Fear and Loathing in Las Vegas*, all wrapped up in a monster hunt with your friends and a lot of beer, and you'll get the picture.

To his credit, Scott steered clear of doing an in-depth, case-by-case analysis of the Bigfoot controversy (in a particularly amusing scene, he decides to avoid a multi-mile-trek through the woods to the scene of the Patterson film purely because it would mean having to take some exercise), and instead delivered a unique slice of Americana in a fashion that few had successfully achieved. Always fun, informative, and thought-provoking, and produced by someone with a passion and a great affection for his subject matter, both DVDs are essential viewing. And for me, they still are, not at least for the fact that I got to meet (on-screen, at least) Scott's girlfriend, mom and dad, and his pet dog, the latter playing an integral and crucially important role in Scott's valiant attempts to utilize high-tech camera wizardry as a part of his Sasquatch quest.

On the following day, we all headed off for a boat-trip to the genuinely spooky-looking Caddo Lake, which was but a short drive from Jefferson. Caddo Lake happens to be the largest natural freshwater lake in the south, covering approximately 26,800 acres. Originally home to the Caddo Indians, a friendly and peaceful tribe that hunted, fished, and made pottery, the lake's murky depths and incredibly dense black cypress trees help to create a truly spooky atmosphere within which Bigfoot firmly thrives. And make no mistake: Encounters with North America's most famous man-beast abound at Caddo Lake.

It was around lunchtime when all of the speakers and their partners arrived at the lake, and we hired a two-level boat that took us on a 90-minute trip around its darkened waters. Even under the glare of the harsh Texas sun, it was easy to determine how different things would be at night after darkness had descended upon those cypress trees. One of those convinced that Bigfoot inhabited the lake was Charlie DeVore, who had lived on Big Cypress Bayou since 1990. Charlie had spent a large amount of time searching for the beast, and, on several occasions, had come across an overpowering stench in the area that he firmly believed to be the creature's scent: "Bigfoot no longer scares me. It might if one was standing right over me, but they've never hurt anybody," said DeVore, adding: "It exists. Too many people have seen it. It exists."

And DeVore's encounters were far from isolated. From the files of the Gulf Coast Bigfoot Research Organization came the following, summer 1984 report: "I was just a young kid then, but I used to go to a summer camp every summer near Caddo Lake. What happened was I was playing with some other kids, near a wooded area, and one of them said, 'Look.' I looked and saw a face looking at us thru some thick bush. It had both hands on either side of its face holding apart a path for it to view us. It quickly leaned back and let the branches go, and that was the last we saw of it...it had a big head, was light brown in color, had big dark hollow looking eyes, a large broad nose, not a flat nose, but broad. It was probably about 7- to 8-foot off the ground and it seemed to have a look of curiosity on its face."

Similarly, Craig Woolheater acknowledged that "a lot of things" had happened at the lake in the 1960s, and that in the 1970s, a beast known as the Caddo Critter was seen roaming the tree-shrouded lake. After returning to the shore, it was time for us all to say our goodbyes, and Dana and I headed back to Dallas—to await the next bout of bizarreness.

11

Ghost Lights and Spooky Lights

As 2004 drew to a close, Dana and I flew to England to celebrate Christmas with my family, and we then headed off to the wilds of Scotland to bring in the New Year with two friends of ours, Ian and Liz, who lived in the picturesque, ancient city of Aberdeen. Indeed, this was the same Ian with whom I had flown to the Laughlin UFO Congress in March 2001. It was the first time that Dana and I had seen him since that weeklong event, and so it was a time of fun and rekindling old friendships over a few pints of good old British beer by the warmth of a stone fireplace.

I cannot say that anything truly strange occurred during the course of our three weeks in Britain (unless, that is, you include the look on Dana's face on New Year's Eve when she saw for the first time what a Scotsman wears under his kilt—nothing). Not that I minded, though: It was Christmas, and it was a time of celebration and for catching up with family, with friends, and for celebrating the season of goodwill. But it wasn't long before I was once again immersed in strangeness. Indeed, the year began with me descending into the flooded depths of a haunted cellar at the request of Las Vegas magicians Penn & Teller. Midway through 2005, I truly became Public Enemy Number One in the eyes of the UFO research community. The fall saw me back on the island of Puerto Rico again, and once more chasing the deadly Chupacabras. I ended the year running wildly through the now-deserted corridors of two U.S. Air Force bases in search of dead aliens and spectral snakes. A pretty good 12 months, I thought.

It was in early January that the researcher, who had hired me for the Sci Fi Channel's *Proof Positive* series, phoned me with yet another out-of-this-world offer. It transpired that he was no longer with *Proof Positive*, but was now working for Showtime on the wonderfully named *Bullshit*, which was basically a televised excuse for its hosts, the aforementioned Penn & Teller, to try and make themselves look amusing and clever by poking fun at those invited to partake in the show. They were offering a decent fee, and an expenses-paid weekend trip to the south's most haunted town, so I obligingly agreed to go along for the ride. That most of my investigations revolved around cryptozoology and UFOs, and that I knew next-to-nothing about ghosts, mattered not in the slightest to the *Bullshit* crew.

Also along for that same ride was Texas-based ghost hunter and paranormal expert Lisa Farwell, who I had met for lunch in Austin some months previously. Our location was all too familiar to me. It was Jefferson, Texas: home to both Dana's aunt Jeannie and the annual conference of the Texas Bigfoot Research Group.

"We've got you booked into a bed-and-breakfast in town," said the researcher when, a few days later, he called me back.

"Is it Jeannie Tatum's place?" I asked, somehow already knowing what the answer was going to be.

"Er, yes, it is," he replied somewhat suspiciously, and inquired: "How did you know that?" Doubtless thoughts were running wildly around his head to the effect that I had somehow managed to hack my way into the highly secret computer banks at *Bullshit* HQ.

"Oh, Jeannie's my wife's aunt, and I was there a few months ago for a Bigfoot conference; all the speakers stayed at her place. I figured you would pick there. So she's gone from Bigfoot to ghosts. Not bad for a bed-and-breakfast in Texas." I added: "Weird shit like this follows me all the time."

He, similar to Craig Woolheater several months previously when he had been placed in a similar situation, was momentarily flummoxed, but soon recovered his usual, laid-back calm self when he realized that nothing untoward was afoot. And so, a date was formulated for a weekend in February. On a Thursday evening, I traveled a couple of hours to Jefferson with the show's producer, who had flown in from Los Angeles, and thereafter met the crew, one of who, a freelancer from Dallas, was the absolute spitting image of late-night talk-show host Conan O'Brien.

Before we began filming some head-and-shoulder footage at Jeannie's on the Friday afternoon, a minor scuffle broke out concerning the nature of my attire. I wanted to wear a Johnny Ramone t-shirt, as a tribute to the mighty guitarist who had died after a five-year battle against prostate cancer the previous September. The producer, however, was having none of it, and said that to see Johnny's scowling face, bowl-haircut, and low-strung guitar on *Bullshit* would be construed as "advertising." And Showtime's lawyers would have none of that, I was firmly told.

"Fine," I replied, as I went upstairs to change into a plain, black t-shirt. "But I'm still wearing my leather jacket." Then, after that particular piece of filming was concluded, we hastily headed into town. Situated on the Big Cypress Bayou, Jefferson has a long and rich history. During the Civil War, the people of Jefferson played a vital role in providing the Confederate Army with meat, hides, food samples, iron, munitions, and leather goods. But it was the years after the War that saw Jefferson really begin to shine, when hundreds of people from the devastated southern states poured into town, all seeking a new life.

By 1872, the Bayou was busy with exports in the thousands, with literally tons of wool, pelts, and bushels of seed, cattle, sheep, and lumber all pouring out of Jefferson, ensuring its people a steady income. It would only be a short while later, however, that that the situation would drastically change when the U.S. Corps of Engineers decided, in its infinite wisdom, to drop the water level in the Big Cypress Bayou, the effect being that ship's crews refused to negotiate the now-hazardous waters. And coupled with the advent of the railroads, Jefferson fell into decline for years. But there was good news, as the town's official Website noted:

> Today, Jefferson is a quaint small town featuring tour attractions reminiscent of its heyday. Its streets are lined with antique and gift shops stocked with unique treasures. Horse-drawn carriages and trolleys tour along the original brick streets. Just one block away from downtown are riverboat tours of Big Cypress Bayou, the same waterway once traveled by stern-wheelers. Evenings in town offer live theater productions, as well as a variety of dining choices. Retiring for the night in Jefferson offers the opportunity to experience any of the over 60 bed and breakfast establishments, including the Excelsior Hotel.

The Excelsior was certainly a glorious hotel, but it was the nearby Jefferson Hotel that we had our sights set on. Indeed, the place was a veritable hotbed of ghostly activity, the staff was keen to tell us. And having recognized that ghosts + spooky hotel = tourists, the Jefferson Hotel proudly paraded its supernatural inhabitants to one and all. As the hotel's own Website noted:

> ...there is the story of a couple in Room 5 whose young son awakened them repeatedly because a man in a long coat and high boots would not go away. Whispers and repetitive knocks are common occurrences. At times there is a thick white cloud with a thin, long-haired blonde in the mist. She seems to be emotionally attached to a bed that was moved from Room 12 to Room 14. A 90-year-old man reluctantly told his tale of wandering the hotel at 1 a.m. after not being able to sleep. He saw the petite blonde

woman floating down the stairs smiling at him, only to disappear before she reached the bottom step. He said he never believed in ghosts until he saw her!

In other words, the Jefferson Hotel was a veritable hotbed of ghostly activity. And, with all of that going on, we could not afford to miss a chance to hang out in some of the hotel's most-haunted rooms. The crew filmed endless shots of us wandering around the hotel with ghost-hunting equipment such as cameras, infrared gear, motion detectors, and a variety of other gadgets. But despite hours of traipsing along the corridors, and catching the alarmed glances of guests who were wondering why on Earth a pale and pasty-looking English guy with a shaved head and biker jacket was roaming the hotel's corridors on his hands and knees—at midnight, no less—with a weird, brightly lit box in his hand, the spirits of Jefferson failed to show up. But soon we were bound for our next location: a supposedly haunted, and abandoned, old building with a grimy old cellar. Somehow, I just knew that I was going to end up in that cellar. And, indeed, my suspicions proved to be correct.

The dark streets of Jefferson were well and truly empty by now; and, as we strolled around with no one but ourselves and old, 19th-century hotels and stores for company, I almost mused upon the possibility that Lisa and I had taken a step through some strange gateway into the past. That is, until I heard the producer shout: "Nick, Lisa: cameras are rolling."

And so we made our way to the spooky, old, abandoned building that was situated just off the main street, and where I was required to perform for my supper, or, I should say, where I was required to perform for my dollars, food, and drinks. We turned the key, and the creaking door slowly opened. "Keep going, keep going," the producer urged.

"Nick," asked the producer, "can you lift up the metal cover?" as he pointed to a large, round, iron lid of some sort that sat atop a raised part of the floor. Ah yes, I thought, this is the access point to the underground lair that everyone is so enamored with. And I was right. The next step was to film me racing to grab a conveniently situated ladder, which I then lowered into the ink-black darkness after removing the cover. With the camera forever rolling, I slowly descended the creaking ladder, step-by-step. What would I find down here? Skeletons? The remains of a deranged unfortunate who had been chained to the wall a century earlier? Buried treasure? A secret code written on the walls? Nothing so spectacular, unfortunately.

As I finally vanished beneath the floor level, I turned on my flashlight to find that the cellar, which I estimated to have a ceiling height of about 15 feet, was flooded with about 10 feet of filthy, stinking water. There was no treasure, unfortunately, but there were plenty of beer cans, used condoms, and candy wrappers floating around. And there *was* a message on the wall, but it was no secret code. Rather it read *Chris Loves Shanna, 4/1/04*. Presumably that was 2004 and not 1904. But again, I dutifully performed for the cameras and waved my flashlight around wildly as the crew loomed over me.

"Excellent!" cried the director. "We're done." And indeed, we were. I hauled myself out of the cellar, walked out into the cold, dark night, collected my check, and left behind me the ghosts, ghouls, and specters of old Jefferson.

In May 2005, a synchronicity of strange proportions occurred when, exactly four years after me, Dana, Jon Downes, and Richard Freeman were hanging out at the Edenfield Hotel in Lytham St. Anne's, England, where the annual LAPIS UFO Conference was held, a strange creature was seen in the same area—and within literal spitting distance of the driveway of the hotel. Under the headline *The Beast of Lytham*, the following story appeared in the British national newspaper, the *Daily Mail* on May 6:

> Dubbed The Beast of Green Drive, the mysterious creature has been spotted roaming in thick woodland at a beauty spot. About as tall as a collie dog but with huge ears, a large mouth and a lolloping gait, the peculiar animal has caused a frenzy of chatter in the normally sedate Lytham St Anne's, Lancashire. The creature, according to witnesses, is seen mainly in the largely wooded area of Green Drive, where there is plenty of brush and scrub to conceal a large animal.

Sandra Sturrock, who was walking her dog when she came face-to-face with the beast, said: "I caught sight of something large ahead of us. It was like a large collie, light in color with large, sticking-up ears. It was watching me and my dog. I stood completely still for several minutes trying to see it more closely. I called my dog and put him on the leash and slowly inched toward the animal to get a better look but it ran off. I then went to where it had been, and my dog went mad, sniffing all round the area. I have never seen anything like this before. I lived in Cheshire for 10 years and frequently saw foxes and the odd deer. They usually disappear quite quickly and do not remain watching you."

Willie Davidson, a house painter, was another witness to the strange beast: "I was playing bowls near Green Drive when I heard a snarl behind me. It was like a monster out of *Doctor Who* and it needs tracking down." A further source, who did want to be named, said: "I was walking along the drive when I saw it in the fields alongside. I have no idea what it was. I could tell it was the size of a Labrador, but looked more like a hare. It can't have been either. It was surreal."

One theory suggested that the beast was a Muntjac deer, one of the last remaining from a herd brought to Lytham Hall by the local squire over a century before. However, the description of the creature looking like "a monster" out of the popular British sci-fi series *Doctor Who* inspired very little faith in the idea that the animal was merely a deer.

A spokesman for Lancashire Police said at the time: "We have checked local zoos and farms, but nothing seems to be missing. It is very bizarre. We have handed it over to the RSPCA to investigate." Experts at Chester Zoo were baffled after being shown the drawing of the Beast of Green Drive. A spokesman said last night: "It does not look like any mammal currently alive. It looks more like a mythical beast to us." The mystery remained precisely that.

In early 2005, Rob Riggs, author of the book *In the Big Thicket*, who I had first met in the summer of 2003, telephoned me and asked if I would be interested in speaking at a summer conference he was planning on holding in the city of Austin, Texas, on the subject of "ghost lights," and the links between that same phenomenon and sacred sites, stone circles, and Bigfoot-like entities. I replied that, yes, I would definitely be interested.

And thus was born the Texas Ghost Lights Conference that was held at, of all places, Austin's First Unitarian Universalist Church on Saturday, June 11. Precisely what the God-fearing folk of the Church thought about a group of Bigfoot-hunting, ghost-light-seeking adventurers descending upon their property, I never learned. But they evidently didn't seem to mind. In addition to Rob and me, the other lecturers were Jim Bunnell and Paul Devereux. Jim had an interesting background: the author of two books on the famous Marfa Lights, namely *Night Orbs* and *Seeing Marfa Lights*, he was an aeronautical and mechanical engineer by profession, and had retired in 2000 from BAE Systems as Director of Mission Solutions for various U.S. Air Force programs.

Similar to me, Paul was a Brit, and he was a long-standing, prestigious figure in the field of ghost-light style phenomena, and a renowned author, too. I had never met Paul before, and I confess that I thought he was probably going to be a bit of a stuffy, college professor-type. But I could not have been more off target if I had tried. Very down-to-earth and with a fine sense of humor, Paul was a pleasure to be around and ensured that we had smiles on our faces at all times. The packed audience was highly receptive to the presentations, as evidenced by the line of questioning that followed the event. But it was what was in store after the conference that I was looking forward to.

In addition to organizing the conference, Rob had also put into place something that he termed the *Bragg Road Project*. Essentially, it was a road trip to the Big Thicket that he had planned for the day after the Austin gig. The idea was to travel down to the woods of east Texas and hang out in the area for two nights, in the event that something—be it a ghost light or a Bigfoot, or both if we were that lucky—decided to make an appearance.

And so early on what turned out to be a fabulously sunny Sunday morning, Rob; Jim; Paul; Miles Lewis of the Austin-based Scientific Anomaly Institute; and two conference attendees, Renee and Nancy; and I met at a prearranged location for our journey into the unknown. I can hardly say that the trip was one of proportions that would have made Jack Kerouac proud. Nevertheless, we were on a mission and everyone was fired up about what we might uncover, and so our convoy set off in earnest. It was late afternoon when we finally arrived in the town of Kountze, where all of us had reservations at the local *Super 8 Motel*. And after a brief shower and a Mexican dinner, we were forest-bound. And this was where, as was so often the case, things got very strange.

Bragg Road can be an eerie location during daylight, as I had found it so when I ventured deep into the Big Thicket with Rob in the summer of 2003. At night and under the spotlight of a full moon, however, it was truly spooky. Not in a scary sense, as I always relished the opportunity to check out such places, but just from the perspective of believing that quite possibly *anything* could happen here—and it did.

Crammed into several all-terrain vehicles, and amid mountains of fold-out chairs, tables, flashlights, bottled-water, snacks, cameras, and a vast array of high-tech recording equipment, we negotiated the moonlit road with extreme care, for one prime reason: The dirt floor of Bragg Road was covered with a heavy layer of dust that was surely 3 or 4 inches thick. As a result, in no time at all our vehicles were literally covered with the offending substance, and the fact that it swirled around so violently as we were driving made it appear that we were trying to negotiate a huge, and practically impenetrable, fog-bank. Every so often the overhanging, twisted limbs of a large tree would penetrate the dust and loom into view like the elongate claw of some vile, nightmarish creature, only to vanish again, back into the swirling storm. But finally, we reached our location: a stretch of the road that was about 4 miles deep within the woods, and where there was room for us to park and make a camp.

Having done so, and with flashlights in hand, we began a walk through the darkened woods, with Rob pointing out to us various locations where wild men, alleged surviving pockets of Native American Indians, Bigfoot, and, of course, ghost lights, had been seen and reported for decades. For 20 minutes or so, we walked around, seemingly forever trying to avoid the overwhelming mass of mosquitoes that surrounded us, while at the same time negotiating the thick blanket of ancient and mighty trees that dominated the area. And then, suddenly, it happened.

We were on our way back to the vehicles to grab a bite to eat and some drinks when, as we entered a clearing in the trees, a basketball-sized bright light floated over us at a height of about 35 feet. It was moving from right to left, and sailed slowly, yet, purposefully on its journey. The ghost light was present for barely 10 seconds, but I managed to quickly capture the strange visitor on

Ghost Light Road after the sun has set, and the beasts of the night begin to surface.

camera before it blinked out, never to return. Indeed, it all happened so fast that I almost convinced myself it had merely been a dream or the result of wishful thinking. But it was neither. The photograph had clearly recorded the ghost light. And more importantly, several members of the group could be seen in the picture, too, as could the road and the surrounding trees. In other words, I had secured an almost perfectly framed image of one of the Big Thicket's mysterious ghost lights.

We kept vigil until around 4 a.m. and caught occasional glimpses of similar lights, albeit of a smaller size, flitting through the trees, taunting and mocking us almost, and daring us to follow them into the heart of the woods, which I did, but to no avail. Like true specters, one second they were there and the next they were gone. This strange spectacle continued throughout the early hours of the morning, and I recall saying to Rob, just as we were about to leave around 4 a.m., that if Bigfoot itself had turned up right about then I would not have been surprised. Maybe I shouldn't have made such a joke, though, because on the following night something even stranger than my ghost light sighting occurred. Unfortunately, I was not there to see it, as I had planned to visit a guy named Gerald who lived in a nearby town, and who had a fascinating tale to tell about how he had seen a large ape-like animal roaming the area decades earlier.

And so, on the following afternoon, and after we had all grabbed a few hours sleep after the previous night's excursions, I said my goodbyes to Rob, Paul, and the rest of the team, and headed off in search of my interviewee.

Gerald was a no-nonsense guy, who had worked in a Port Arthur refinery for years, and who lived a short journey from Kountze. Two days before the interview he had turned 60 years old; and as he sat in his recliner surrounded by birthday cards, while we drank iced tea, he related to me the facts of his strange experience of three decades earlier.

According to Gerald, his encounter had occurred in June 1977, interestingly enough, around the witching hour, when he was driving through Kountze and close to the town's Old Hardin Cemetery. Suddenly, his car's engine began to falter and its lights faded. Gerald, thinking that perhaps a fuse was to blame, carefully brought the vehicle to a halt at the side of the road. However, as he exited the vehicle to take a look under the hood, at a distance of perhaps 50 or 60 feet from him, Gerald saw a tall, and very skinny, dark, hair-covered figure walking across the road, "like a man but leaning forward and swinging [its] arms."

The sighting only lasted a few seconds, recalled Gerald, and the creature vanished into the trees. But most notable was what happened next: Only two or three seconds later, a soccer ball-sized, glowing mass of bright light came floating through the trees at a height of about 50 or 60 feet, and from the exact spot where the creature had vanished into the woods. The ghost light moved slowly across the road until it was lost from sight amid the thick trees on the opposite side of the road. Interestingly, after both the beast and the light had vanished, Gerald's car started normally and bore no signs of any similar problem again. I thanked Gerald for the interview, and drank the rest of my iced tea. He, in return, tipped his baseball cap in my direction in complete silence and, with a smile, motioned me to the door. I went on my way, pleased that my days were never normal.

When I finally got back to Dallas and turned on the computer, I read a report from Rob that was of true jaw-dropping quality. The odd experiences of the first night in the Big Thicket were apparently not isolated. Indeed, as darkness fell on the second evening, and while I was interviewing Gerald, all hell, metaphorically speaking, had broken loose in the Big Thicket. As Rob said:

> Renee had a frightening experience Monday night. We split up into teams of two and spread out about a mile apart. Renee was paired with Nancy. Nancy walked down the road briefly away from Renee. Renee said she then heard something walking in the woods off the road directly

behind her that sounded large. She said whatever it was, it was large enough to snap twigs, and she said that it seemed to be moving stealthily, as if it were trying to sneak up on her. She panicked, locked herself into her van and drove off, leaving Nancy to fend for herself.

Several hours later she was still shaken and still had goose bumps. Such irrational panic is not characteristic of Renee. She is a ghost hunter and has many times been in creepier situations than being on Bragg Road. She has even gone to cemeteries alone just to test her mettle. There are theories that the creatures deliberately provoke such panic reactions through chemicals in their scent or by mental projection of energy.

Renee, Nancy, and I also saw a peculiar light. It looked somewhat like a firefly but actually left a solid streak 10 to 15 feet in length that was brilliant bluish-white in color. It happened near a power line, and it was suggested that it might have been some kind of surge on the power line itself. But what could cause such a surge? That, in itself, would be suggestive of an electro-magnetic anomaly.

Rob's report was fascinating. In many ways the story it told closely, and very eerily, paralleled the situation that I had found myself in at the Cannock Chase woods in England in 2001, when I, too, encountered what seemed to be shadowy, man-like entities that had the ability to induce intense and disturbing feelings in those that were fortunate enough (or unfortunate enough depending on your perspective), to come into close contact with them. And the fact that the beasts of the Big Thicket were manifesting themselves specifically to people that were looking for them, was another factor that mirrored the events at the Cannock Chase four years earlier. Again, this only served to reinforce my conclusions that the man-beasts of this world were not the flesh-and-blood entities that many cryptozoologists assumed them to be.

Twice, now, I have been to the Big Thicket, and on each occasion I was touched by the hand of high strangeness. I know that, one day, I will, once again, venture deep into the heart of those sinister, ancient woods. Whatever awaits me: Bigfoot, Wild Man, or ghost light, as always I will be ready for it—and, I suspect, it for me.

12

Public Enemy Number One

On June 21, 2005, my book, *Body Snatchers in the Desert: The Horrible Truth at the Heart of the Roswell Story*, was published offering a theory for the notorious 1947 "UFO crash" at Roswell, New Mexico which, until then, had only been quietly, and darkly, hinted at in books and periodicals. The theory centered upon the claims of a variety of military and intelligence old-timers that the Roswell legend was borne out of: (a) a series of shocking and diabolical experiments using physically handicapped people in high-altitude-balloon experiments; and (b) tests connected to early research in the field of nuclear-powered aircraft.

Until that point, I had a fairly good relationship with the E.T. believers within the UFO research community. And for many years I, too, was an adherent of the theory that aliens were among us and had the misfortune, or the bad-driving skills, to crash at Roswell. And, indeed, even with Roswell no longer valid, in my mind at least, as an extraterrestrial event I still held—and still do hold—the view that we have a genuine UFO presence among us that is of unknown origins. However, the research community raised hell when my book was published, and, almost overnight, I became Public Enemy Number One, as is evidenced by the somewhat farcical series of events that occurred after the publication of the book. I should have known that something like this was going to happen though; just such a scenario had been eerily prophesized months before by researcher and author Greg Bishop.

In March 2005, I had flown to Los Angeles to be interviewed for a television documentary that the History Channel was making called *UFO Hunters*. As L.A. was the hometown of Greg, we arranged to meet for dinner at the hotel I was staying in, and then went out on the town with his girlfriend, Sigrid. Greg brought along with him a copy of his latest UFO book, *Project Beta*, and duly signed it for me: "Nick: Soon to be the most unpopular man in Ufology!" Yes, Greg was quite the prophet. Perhaps I should consider asking him to select my lottery numbers?

Three months later, and right around the time that *Body Snatchers* surfaced, I began to hear rumors that a booklet was in circulation titled *Who's Who in UFOs and ETs: The Need for Discernment*, and it featured the wise words of an extraterrestrial named Baktar who was reportedly "speaking through" one Nicholette Pavlevsky, "in response to questions asked by Greg Wright." So those same rumors went, the booklet was alleging dark things about me. Well, of course, I had to pick up a copy as soon as possible.

As luck would have it, Ken Cherry of the Dallas-Fort Worth MUFON group had booked the intrepid pair of Pavlevsky and Wright, and, let us not forget, Baktar, too, to deliver the monthly lecture at the group's May 2005 meeting, which was held in a small library, about 10 miles from where Dana and I lived. And so, settled in my seat, and with a copy of the booklet now in my possession, I read what the pair was saying about me. I was amused to see that the authors had very carefully stated in the beginning of their tome that, "The information about people and ETs in this book is given according to the perceptions of Baktar (or occasionally other entities) as filtered through the perceptions of a human channel. As such, it may or may not be accurate. It is the privilege and the responsibility of each individual to make their own determination about what they choose to believe." Indeed.

And with that helpful note out of the way, I sat back to read what Baktar knew about me that I evidently didn't:

> Nick Redfern: This author of *The BBI Files* [It was *The FBI Files*, guys. Got it? If that data came from Baktar please see that he is severely punished for his heinous crime] and *Cosmic Crashes* is a disinformer for the power-elite connected black military....The black clothes he wears, as worn by judges, preachers, and police officers, project doom and power, and doom *because* of the power.

Yes, it was, and still is, quite true that I like to wear black and not much else. So does my monster-hunting friend, Richard Freeman. And, so what, Baktar? The simple explanation is indeed the correct one: I wear black because I like to wear black. And I can honestly say that I never thought that by wearing black I was conveying an atmosphere of power and doom. But in the UFO game, you can never please everyone. Not that I care in the slightest about pleasing people, anyway. I promptly forgot the amusing claims, and thought about what I was going to eat for dinner later that night.

And then there were the e-mails that arrived after I had been interviewed by George Noory on *Coast-to-Coast* in the early hours of June 22, 2005, on the subject of *Body Snatchers*. The interview did not finish until 4 a.m., and so I slept in until lunchtime the next day. But after I finally crawled out of bed, I was pleasantly surprised to find about 170 e-mails in my inbox from people who had listened to the show. For the most part, the e-mails were eerily similar: "YOU ARE A FUCKING IDIOT!" wrote one sane and rational soul in bold capitals. "You are full of shit and you know it," said another. A third accused me of being on the payroll of the Illuminati; and a fourth, somewhat bizarrely, asked me if I was telling such "lies" to appease my reptilian masters who provided me with buxom sex slaves from South America. I wrote back saying that it actually was true that I had a buxom sex slave, but she was from Nederland, Texas, not South America. I got no response to that one. I duly printed all of the offending e-mails and placed them into a folder that I titled in black marker: *The Fucking Idiot Who is Full of Reptilian Shit File*. My rather unique fan mail from maniacal oddballs still languishes within the folder to this day. A popular man, I most certainly was not.

Then in the August/September issue of *UFO Magazine*, columnist Steve Bassett wrote an article titled *Words and Metaphors*, which amused me when I read that my name was included in a list of "Men (and Women) in Gray," who Bassett described as "working or [who] have worked in government service...and [who] are engaging extraterrestrial-related phenomena and exopolitics in the public arena." Imagine my surprise when I read that, according to Bassett, I had a background in the British Air Force.

This was the fourth or fifth time since the publication of *Body Snatchers* that someone was claiming that I was, or had been, on a government payroll. Some people had even alluded to the possibility that I was being paid large sums of dollars by the Pentagon, in return for saying that nothing of an extraterrestrial nature crashed at Roswell. It was all absolute nonsense, though, as I told *UFO Magazine* in a response letter to the Bassett article:

> I truly wish I could claim to have a cool, fighter-pilot-style background, soaring among the clouds and blasting the crap out of the bad guys, but, sadly, reality is far more down to earth. Needless to say, I have no military or government background of any kind at all (although my father served in the British Royal Air Force, where he worked as a radar mechanic).
>
> As far as my background is concerned, these are the facts: After completing my education, I worked for two

> years as a feature writer for a British rock music magazine. When that dried up, I worked variously for a couple of years as a van driver, a fork-lift truck driver, a house painter, a shelf stacker, a petrol [gas] pump attendant, an assistant manager in a paint and wallpaper warehouse, and, lowest of the low and much to my everlasting regret, a life-insurance salesman. I went back to writing in my mid-20s, which I have done ever since, primarily on issues totally unrelated to UFOs or anything even remotely paranormal or mysterious.
>
> Doubtless the "fact" that I have a "British Air Force" background will now be seen as evidence by some that I am some form of sinister character wildly dispensing disinformation to the ufological masses, as has, in fact, already been suggested with regard to my book *Body Snatchers in the Desert*.

And in a less-than-veiled reference to the mighty Baktar, I added:

> I've even seen truly bizarre published references within the UFO community to the effect that, since I usually only wear black (primarily T-shirts, jeans, and leather biker jackets), this makes me again somewhat sinister. *Sigh*.

I signed off: "Nick 'Top Gun' Redfern." To his credit, Steve Bassett apologized and admitted that he had received faulty data about me from that fountain of truth and reliability known as the Internet.

13

The Goat-Man Cometh

It is somewhat ironic that the one investigation that I suspected would prove to be almost certainly fruitless in terms of securing anything even remotely tangible evidence-wise, actually turned out to be one of the most intriguing of all my excursions into the realm of the unknown. If I needed reminding, it taught me a valuable lesson: Never assume anything. And, in July 2005, after trekking through the woods surrounding Lake Worth, Texas, with the former lead singer of a band called the Bozo Porno Circus, in search of a creature described as being half man and half goat, I certainly don't.

Before I get into the heart of the quest, some essential background on the beast of Lake Worth is required. It was in the early morning hours in the summer of 1969 that six terrified Fort Worth residents headed breathlessly for their local police station and told a remarkable tale. John Reichart, his wife, and two other couples were parked at Lake Worth, at the witching hour, no less, when an unholy beast that sounded like it had emerged from the foul, stinking depths of some Lovecraftian nightmare leaped out of the buckling branches of a nearby tree. Covered, curiously, in both fur and scales, it slammed with an almighty bang onto the hood of the Reicharts' vehicle and tried to "grab" the hysterical Mrs. Reichart, before bounding off into the endless darkness and the cover of the thick woods. Its only telltale calling card: an 18-inch-long scratch along the side of the car.

Although this particular incident quickly gathered widespread publicity, and was taken very seriously by the police—no less than four units were dispatched to the scene—it was not the first time that the authorities had heard dark tales of weird things lurking within the heart of the woods of Lake Worth. For no less than eight weeks, sightings of a strange animal had been quietly discussed among the superstitious locals, and the police kept a careful watch on the unfolding drama, preferring to attribute the reports to the work of juvenile pranksters, rampaging around in ape costumes. Not an impossible scenario; but, having come to know how gun-happy the residents of little Texan towns can be, any practicing prankster must have had a real death wish.

Patrolman James S. McGee admitted that the report filed by John Reichart was treated with the utmost seriousness because "those people were really scared." Indeed, such was the interest that the case generated, it became the subject of a high-profile article in the *Fort Worth Star Telegram* written by none other than Jim Marrs, who would find fame in later years with his numerous books on subjects such as UFOs, the JFK assassination, and 9/11.

Fishy Man-Goat Terrifies Couples Parked at Lake Worth was the headline that jumped out of the pages of the *Telegram*. And of course, it made the Goat-Man a household name in the closely-knit neighborhood. Perhaps inevitably, within 24 hours the Goat-Man was seen again. Once more, it was around midnight and a report came in of the beast crossing a road near the Lake Worth Nature Center. Notably, the witness, Jack Harris of Fort Worth, said that as he tried to photograph the animal, his camera flash failed. As seasoned cryptozoologists will be aware, even if it is something that many of them prefer not to talk about, malfunctioning cameras are a staple part of encounters with mysterious animals, reinforcing the theory that at least some of these entities may have paranormal origins or abilities.

The creature was then seen to quickly make its way to the top of a nearby bluff, with 30 to 40 people in hot pursuit. In fact, the scenario eerily paralleled that of the old Frankenstein movies of the 1930s and 1940s, which saw the unfortunate creation pursued by torch-wielding maniacs from some isolated European town. But the Goat-Man had a surprise for them: Looming over them at a height of about 30 feet, it threw a large tire at the crowd that sailed through the air, or bounced along the ground, depending on which version of events you accept as genuine, for an astonishing distance of no less than 500 feet. Perhaps not surprisingly, at that point, said Jack Harris, "everybody jumped back into their cars" and fled the area. That fine Texas spirit of shoot-first-and-ask-questions-later had abruptly and curiously vanished.

Additional reports poured in. Some described the animal as having dark-colored fur, others said that its coat was white, and that it appeared to weigh in the region of 300 pounds. One group of thrill-seekers claimed that they saw the beast break the thick limb of a huge oak tree, and there were even those that were said to have heard its "pitiful cry." More tales of the beast's apparent liking for jumping onto car hoods surfaced, along with reports of sheep having been mutilated and killed in the same area under very weird circumstances. And then there were the theories that the creature had made its lair on a small piece of land on the lake called Greer Island, which was connected to the mainland by a small pathway.

The controversy was reaching fever-pitch level when Helmuth Naumer, of the Fort Worth Museum of Science and History, surfaced with the theory that the Goat-Man was something else entirely: a decidedly down-to-earth pet bobcat that someone had released into Lake Worth Park, and that had a particular fondness for jumping onto cars. Precisely how the bobcat was able to propel a tire 500 feet through the air was never quite explained, however. And Naumer's theory, that could perhaps have been the answer for some of the reports, at least, did not explain the truly bizarre photograph taken by local dress-shop owner Allen Plaster, who caught on film a large, white-colored creature with a body that almost looked like it was made of hundreds of cotton-balls, and atop which sat a ridiculously small head. And while rumors circulated to the effect that the police had caught some pranksters parading around in ape costumes, ultimate verification for this theory was not forthcoming at the time, and the matter was never really resolved to everyone's satisfaction. Therefore, it was inevitable: 36 years later it was time for a new investigation.

I first met Ken Gerhard at the 2003 Crypto Conference of renowned Texas monster hunter, Chester Moore. He cut a striking pose, with his all-in-black gear, his black-leather cowboy hat, and mohawk. We chatted briefly about our collective research, music, and more, and went our separate ways. I would next meet Ken, along with his wife, Lori, about 15 months later in Jefferson, at the annual conference of Craig Woolheater's Texas Bigfoot Research

Ken and Lori Gerhard, seekers of all things monstrous.

Group. Both Ken and Lori were deeply passionate about cryptozoology, and in 2004, Ken wrote a superb, self-published book on the subject titled *Monsters Are Real!* Shortly thereafter, he and Lori headed off to the jungles of darkest Belize in search of man-beasts, and where they continued their monstrous pursuits.

Ken and I stayed in touch by e-mail and, with Dana and me in Dallas, and he and Lori in Houston (where they had previously carved a successful career on the rock-music circuit with Bozo Porno Circus), we discussed the possibility of doing some research together. Finally, we had the perfect case to delve into: the Goat-Man of Lake Worth. A date was arranged: Ken and Lori would drive up from Houston late on the evening of Friday, July 15, and we would make an early start the next morning.

At the time, Dana's grandmother, Gloria, had recently undergone leg surgery and was recovering at her Amarillo home that she shared with Dana's mom, Alex. And, not exactly being a fan of cryptozoology, Dana decided it would be much more fun to fly up there to spend time with her family, instead of accompanying me while I hacked my way through the mosquito-infested woods of Lake Worth in pursuit of strange men who looked like goats. "When will he grow up?" Dana sighed to herself, with a smile, as I dropped her off at Dallas' Love Field Airport. "Never!" I proclaimed loudly. We hugged and kissed, I smacked her on the ass, and soon she was airborne and bound for Amarillo.

Four years previously, I had headed off into the unknown with Jon Downes and Richard Freeman on a six-week, alcohol-fueled romp around Britain in pursuit of all things grotesque and bizarre, the details of which I related in my book *Three Men Seeking*

Monsters. One of the most memorable things for me was that the night before our *Three Stooges*-style adventure began, a huge storm of truly apocalyptic proportions hit Jon's home that resulted in a complete power outage. Most bizarre of all, a large crow flew straight into Jon's kitchen window, Kamikaze style. The feathery, bloody mess was both a precursor to, and an indicator of, the distinctly high strangeness that was to follow.

Oddly, around 6 p.m., and as Ken and Lori were driving up to Dallas, I experienced a curious feeling of déjà vu, when the night before embarking on a cryptozoological excursion of infinitely weird proportions, a dark and foreboding storm headed in. Pouring rain and powerful, howling winds battered our windows, and water flooded the streets, as Mother Nature turned what had been a pleasant summer's evening into a veritable deluge, which was surely on par with anything that even Noah himself had to cope with. And then the power went out and I was in darkness.

"Not again," I said out loud, to nobody but myself. There was no suicidal crow this time, but the power stayed off for about two hours, and I sat in our living room surrounded by a multitude of candles that both flickered and cast eerie, creeping shadows across the darkened room, listening on my headphones to the atmospheric tones of Siouxsie and the Banshees. Indeed, I was actually disappointed when power was finally restored shortly before Ken and Lori arrived, around 9 p.m.

I wish I could say that we feasted on a platter of culinary delights and the finest wines, but instead it was a meal of Sonic burgers, Jack 'n' Coke, and Dr. Pepper. But it did the job, and we sat around until the early hours talking about music, about monster hunting, about the joys of doing exactly what we wanted to do in life, and to hell with the rest of the world. We then retired to our respective beds, and next thing I knew it was morning.

The consummate professional, Ken had packed their vehicle with cameras, high-tech recording equipment, and a whole range of assorted gadgetry that was doubtless going to be put to good use. We set off around 10:30 a.m. and, after stopping at a 7-Eleven for sandwiches and drinks, we arrived at Lake Worth around midday.

"Y'all can bet your ass if I see the critter, I'm gonna blow his goddamned head off of his son-of-a-bitch shoulders," raged one friendly native at me, when we stopped for gas in the center of town on our way to the area, and after he engaged me briefly in conversation about what a "Britisher" was doing in Lake Worth. With bits of chewed-up tobacco hanging from the corner of his mouth, he headed off to his truck with a Dr. Pepper in one hand, and a huge wad of beef jerky in the other. As his immense vehicle

The location of the activities of the diabolical Goat-Man.

rumbled onto the highway, I could see that it was emblazoned with a sticker on its rear that read: "You take my gun, I take your head."

It was a blisteringly hot and humid day when we finally reached the lake itself and, after negotiating the tree-enshrouded, dusty road that led to the car park of the Fort Worth Nature Center and Refuge, we filled our backpacks with plenty of water, juice, candy, and sandwiches, and made our way to the Center. If anyone knew anything about the Goat-Man, it would surely be the staff.

"Oh, yes, I know about that," said one of the volunteers at the Center, with a high degree of apprehension in his voice, after we introduced ourselves, and told him that we were there to uncover all that we could about the mysterious man-beast of the lake. I anticipated that we would be given short shrift. However, despite the fact that he declined to speak on the record and have his name preserved for posterity, the man eventually opened up and chatted in a genial fashion about the creature and its nefarious exploits. Or alleged exploits, as he preferred it. Perhaps inevitably, however, he was highly skeptical of the possibility that anything truly anomalous was lurking deep within the woods.

"People can easily get confused," he told us, adding, "There was one time when people said, even the police said, that a lioness was on the loose in the woods; it turned out to be a large Golden Retriever. Me, I think the stories were told by parents to keep their teenaged kids out of the area at night, and then the legend just grew." He did admit, however, that the area took on a weird atmosphere after sunset, and recalled the comments of a number of his colleagues who flatly refused to stay there after darkness had set in and when the creatures of the night began to stir. We thanked him and set off on our journey into the unknown. "If you catch the critter, let us know!" he shouted, as we departed the Center. We promised that we would.

Our next step was to head off to the bluff, where the mighty beast had allegedly launched, 500 feet into the air, a large tire at the marauding crowd that was in hot pursuit of his scaly, furry, goat-like form. Thankfully, and to our everlasting joy, the location had barely changed in 36 years. Indeed, the only real difference was that, just below the ridge where the Goat-Man had thrown the tire there was now a thick growth of bamboo, creating somewhat of an exotic atmosphere.

We proceeded to do some filming at the scene, and Ken and I discussed the case on camera, while Lori handled the recording. For 10 or 15 minutes, we took photographs, followed the trail to where the Goat-Man was seen looming over the crowd, tire in hand, and tried to envisage what things had been like during that hot, mad summer of 1969, when cars of people were careering violently around the darkened roads of the woods in pursuit of their monstrous quarry.

It was then time for our next stop: Greer Island, the reputed lair of the monster itself. Connected to the mainland by a thin stretch of ground, the heavily treed island is an eerie place. Although it was utterly silent, I got the distinct feeling that we were not alone. As we scoured the area, it was almost as if our every move was being watched by the hidden eyes of some hideously diabolical beast. The lack of any attendant background noise only amplified the sound of the ground under our feet, as it crunched from the leaves, twigs, and broken branches that dominated the island's floor. Evidence of the activity of small mammals could be seen everywhere, and the dark waters of the surrounding lake looked like they could hide just about anything within their murky depths. Indeed, having made our way to Greer Island, it was almost as if we had left all civilization behind. And then, in a small clearing on the island, we found something unusual and potentially of great significance: a teepee.

By that, I do not mean a literal teepee of Native American Indian standards. But instead, something far more interesting. It appeared that something had literally torn large, thick branches off of the surrounding trees, and had carefully placed them into a pyramid-style formation in the clearing.

In cryptozoological circles, and specifically in areas of pronounced Bigfoot activity, discoveries of such formations are surprisingly common. Some researchers suggest the possibility that teepees are a type of location-marker, either for the beasts that construct them, or for others of their kind that may wander into the area. Other investigators postulate that the teepees may indicate the boundaries of the territories in which those same beasts roam. Regardless of why, precisely, the teepees are made, it is a recognized fact that where man-beasts are seen, such teepees are seldom far behind. The discovery also suggested to us that if the Goat-Man was some form of Bigfoot-like entity, and that the teepee had been constructed recently, then it was also distinctly possible that the Goat-Man, or its offspring, at least, was *still* roaming the woods of Lake Worth and Greer Island; and, perhaps, keeping a careful watch on us. Even more was to come.

Only a short distance from the teepee was a large area of flattened ground, where it looked like something big and heavy had sat down, along with the remains of a large fish that had obviously been devoured by, well, something. By this time, Ken, Lori, and I were convinced that something truly unusual was afoot. We never expected to find anything like this on Greer Island, and yet here it was, right in front of us, taunting us almost. We took photographs, we filmed the site, and Ken systematically collected the remains of the fish and deposited them into a bag that he carefully sealed for later analysis. We stayed on the island for a while longer, digesting the intriguing data and evidence that we had uncovered, and then headed back to the bluff, where Ken had parked his vehicle.

Our next step was to phone Chester Moore, who had also traveled to Lake Worth several years previously, but who had been denied access to Greer Island, due to the fact that, at the time, the crossing to the island was closed. Chester was fascinated by what we had found, but was unable to partake in our expedition due to the fact that he was shortly thereafter (a) headed to Spain to search for giant catfish; and (b) off to a gig in Germany where the heavy-metal-based band Manowar, who, somewhat ludicrously, insisted on dressing like characters straight out of *Conan the Barbarian*, were due to perform. Chester asked us to keep him informed of anything and everything that we uncovered, and we did.

After we hung up with Chester, it was time for a lunch of sandwiches and Cokes that we had purchased along the way. We then decided to make our way through the woods to the exact location where the Goat-Man had thrown the tire at the astonished and amazed locals all those years before. The first thing that happened was that I got stung by a bee; the second thing was that, as we closed in on where the beast was seen back in 1969, we were confronted by a pile of tires of exactly the type that the Goat-Man had allegedly slung at his less-than-appreciative audience decades previously. But the third thing that I noticed was perhaps most significant of all.

Only a few minutes walk from the darkened woods where the Goat-Man had been seen in 1969, was a trailer park that contained a multitude of trailers, some in good condition, some in the sort of state that you might imagine guests of a typical episode of Jerry Springer inhabiting; and some that might, perhaps, have harbored an unfortunate in-bred of the type that would have fit one of those long-gone "freak"-based circuses of yesteryear.

Was this the answer to the Goat-Man? Was it really some diabolical unfortunate, the horrifying result of too much inbreeding in the local trailer park? Had the beast escaped from its trailer-bound confines? And if so, had it roamed the woods for the last four decades as its toothless mother, sister, and grandmother—who may very well have all been the same person—sought to capture it and return it to the safety of the trailer park? Probably not! But the thought reduced the three of us to fits of laughter, as *Deliverance*-style imagery flooded our collective minds. From there, the conversation plumbed even greater depths of absurdity, as we began addressing the possibility that the Goat-Man was some sort of genetically-modified freak that had escaped from an underground laboratory at Nevada's infamous Area 51.

As the day progressed, the weather deteriorated where the sky turned black and the rain poured in deluge-style proportions.

And with further filming now utterly out of the question, we decided that our stomachs needed filling again, and so we headed for a nearby Mexican restaurant, and then journeyed back to the Dallas apartment that was my and Dana's home, where we sat around discussing the genuinely intriguing discoveries we had made at the lake. Ken and Lori headed back to their home early Sunday morning. It was a job well done.

The teepee, the strange indentations on the ground, and the general history of the man-beast, led us to believe that there was genuine, high strangeness afoot. Whatever the true nature of the Goat-Man, a misidentified Bigfoot, a trailer-borne in-bred, a phantasm of the night, the result of a secret government experiment in genetics that had gone awry, or something else entirely, we came away from our venture convinced of one thing: Not only was something hideous and monstrous lurking within the darkened woods of Lake Worth and Greer Island in 1969, it appeared that it was still there. We vowed to one day return and spend a night out on Greer Island. But the story was not quite over.

Five months later, in December 2005, I traveled to San Bernardino, California, to film the pilot episode of a new series—about which I will tell later. One of those that also appeared on the show was Jim Marrs, who had brought to the world's (well, okay, a small part of Texas's) attention the diabolical exploits of the Goat-Man all those years ago.

When I asked Jim what he thought lay behind the mystery, he answered quickly that, in his opinion, it was all the work of teenagers, running around in ape suits, who were lucky not to get shot or arrested and charged with breaking some obscure, local law. This was certainly not implausible, and indeed such a theory had been advanced at the time. But what of the additional encounters that followed? What about the photographs, and the malfunctioning camera? And most important from my perspective: What about the teepee and the general weirdness on Greer Island that Ken, Lori, and I had discovered? I concluded that even if the initial encounter had been a hoax, the intense, collective belief in the beast at a local level and in the years that followed, may very well have resulted in the creation of a paranormal, Tulpa-like thought-form that still roamed the area in a state of semi-existence, seeking out unfortunate souls, upon whose emotional energy the mind-monster thrived.

There was no doubt in my mind: There was something very strange lurking deep within the woods of Lake Worth.

14

Around the World in 30 Days

The period from August to September 2005 was insanely hectic, even by my standards. In early August, I traveled back to jolly old England for two and a half weeks to attend Jon Downes' annual Weird Weekend conference in the ancient city of Exeter. Hanging out at the Weird Weekend is an unusual experience, to say the least, but no one can ever say that the event is neither fun nor memorable. Steve Jones (the Pagan Witch and magistrate, not the god-like guitarist from the Sex Pistols who shares the same moniker) discussed ghostly Black Dog legends; Richard Freeman pontificated wildly, and shared with the audience his *Indiana Jones*-style escapades of earlier that year while pursuing the monstrous Death Worm of Mongolia; I spoke to a surprisingly highly receptive audience about my down-to-earth theories on

Roswell, as well as my experiences while searching for the Goat-Man; renowned lake monster researcher and author Peter Costello made a rare surfacing; and a multitude of others took their turns to entertain the faithful that had flocked to the haunted 15th-century Cowick Barton pub.

Most of the weekend was spent catching up on the latest news and gossip, and hanging out with Jon and his new girlfriend, Corinna. Oh, yes, I almost forgot: In a question-and-answer competition that was held on the Saturday afternoon, I won a toy "ray gun" attached to which was a 6-inch-long plastic penis that had been thoughtfully placed there by Richard. A friend of Jon's, whose name I will omit to spare her blushes, asked me, while almost salivating in the direction of the toy gun, if she could "have the thing on the end." Definitely not wanting to explain what that same "thing" was to the Customs people at the airport on my return to the States, I obligingly said yes. She delicately took a hold of it, and the last time I saw her (and it) she was quickly heading in the direction of the women's bathroom. As with so many events, and when catching up with old friends until the early hours, the time sadly flew by, and a coach journey back to my dad's house in central England quickly beckoned. But not before I was able to hang out in Jon's bedroom with him watching a video of an ear-splitting performance of *Louie, Louie* that Jon and his band, the Amphibians from Outer Space, had performed at the Weird Weekend the previous year. Jon and I had a riotously hysterical time watching the footage, but then, sadly, it really was time to say goodbye.

Only hours after getting back to my dad's place, I received a call from a Canadian TV company asking if I would be interested in being filmed for a documentary on the Roswell "crashed UFO" controversy. "It'll mean you flying to Monterrey, Mexico in a few days from now," said the urgent voice at the other end of the phone. "But we'll pay your flight, and all your expenses—and give you a bit more, too," I was helpfully and encouragingly told. And so, four days later, after having flown back to Dallas, and having a couple of romantic days and nights with Dana, I was south-of-the-border bound.

I had been to Mexico twice before, on vacation, but this was my first time to Monterrey. I was not disappointed. Having been met at the airport by a man named Armando, whose family was big in the local chocolate-production industry, and who drove at lightning speed, I arrived at my location: a hotel situated on the corner of a courtyard in the heart of the city. After I had dropped my bags off at the hotel, Armando and I strolled across the courtyard to a small restaurant where the crew from Canada—Paul who was the audio expert, Jeff the cameraman, and Robin, the heavily-pregnant producer—were relaxing with nachos and beer. I dove without encouragement into the very welcome morsels, and we sat and got to know each other for an hour or so. Then we were headed for the mountains and the interview.

Robin chose a location high in the hills that was a small, tree-shrouded observatory and which, I suppose, was as good a place as any to undertake an interview on all things Roswellian. Personally, I was just having fun being on an all-expenses-paid trip to Monterrey for two days. After about two hours of filming, we headed back to town. The Canadians had been in Monterrey for a few days, and as a result, Paul had got himself a date that night with a local girl he had met two nights previously. Jeff and Robin were too exhausted to do much at all. And so, I spent a few hours wandering around town. Also, there was a traditional Mexican band playing in the courtyard that night that I decided to check out. I sat, hanging out and listening for a while, soaking in the culture and the climate, and marveling at the architecture and scenery that a person always embraces, or should embrace, when experiencing new worlds and exotic locales.

I was wearing a Ramones t-shirt that night, and a 20-something punk noticed it, came over, and engaged me in conversation. His name was Jose and, thankfully, his English was far better than my embarrassing attempts at Spanish. He told me how he played in a combo that fused traditional Mexican music with hardcore punk, and we sat chatting about bands, about gigs, about soccer, and toasted to the future with a shot of something sweet that came from a small bottle, which Jose kept in the inside pocket of his leather jacket. What it was I do not know, but, by God, it tasted good.

In fact, it may not have been entirely coincidental that only a few hours after drinking the murky liquid, I was fast asleep in my hotel room, having a very vivid out-of-body experience (OBE) that, to this day, I still distinctly recall. It was almost as if I was in a swimming pool, and I would kick my legs against the walls of the room and drift effortlessly across its expanse at a height that varied from about 6 inches above the carpet to around 8 feet. It truly did feel as if I could fly. Bright lights flickered all around me, and a small plant that was situated next to the television swayed gently in my direction as I glided toward it. Whether it was all a dream or a genuine OBE induced by the powers of the demon-liquid of several hours earlier, I never really knew. But morning came all too fast, and the Canadians and I were bound for pastures new. For me, it was Dallas, and for them it was a trip to Puerto Rico to make a show on the Chupacabras. Their guide on the island, they told me, was a woman named Carola, the same Carola, it transpired, who had been Jon Downes' and my guide on behalf of the Sci Fi Channel a year before.

Again, my trip back to Dallas and back to Dana was a brief one, and so we made the most of it. Twenty-four hours after returning to Dallas from Monterrey, I was on a flight to Los Angeles, where I was due to speak at the annual National UFO Conference (NUFOC) in Hollywood. I never say no to speaking engagements at conferences: aside from the fact that they always present a good opportunity to update people on one's current research, many of them pay pretty well, too. And invariably, old friends from the lecture circuit turn up, and late night revelry becomes part and parcel of the occasion. And NUFOC did not disappoint, in any respects.

The NUFOC gigs had, for years, been organized under the auspices of Jim Moseley. However, the reins had been recently transferred to Lisa Davis, who put on a highly professional (but, sadly, vastly under-attended) weekend-long conference that saw numerous familiar faces lurking in the shadows. The *Excluded Middle*'s Greg Bishop was there, as was *Saucer Smear*'s Jim Moseley, radio-host Rob Simone (who, every time I saw him, was doing a loud impression of Arnold Schwarzenegger, and a pretty good one at that), UFO authors Rich Dolan and Linda Howe, flying saucer investigator David Sereda, crop circle researchers Ed Sherwood (a fellow Brit) and his wife, Kris, and a multitude of booksellers peddling their varied wares.

I groaned loudly, but had to smile too, when I saw that the couple who had lectured in Dallas three months before and that had accused me, with deadly seriousness, of being a black-garbed disinformation agent of the secret government was also there. Canadian researcher Grant Cameron was supposed to be there. However, conspiratorial murmurings began to quietly trickle down the ufological grapevine that weekend to the effect that Grant had been "stopped at the border," by U.S. Immigration, and refused him entry on the grounds that he did not have the required work permit that he needed to enter the States. Never mind the fact that he was only going to receive an honorarium from Lisa in return for delivering his lecture, but the robots at Immigration, who, in that tried-and-tested tradition, were "just following orders," cared not a bit, and Grant was sent back home. Whether the result of pathetic bureaucracy or dark conspiracy, the controversy surrounding this admittedly odd affair still resonates within UFO circles to this day.

I always enjoyed—and still do—hanging out with Greg Bishop, as I consider us like-minded souls, who share a passion for music, the Beat authors, and the fun of living a lifestyle that is about as far away from normality as it is possible for a person to get. As Greg had noted, after the controversy, flak and outrage that his then recent book *Project Beta* had brought him, and that my *Body Snatchers in the Desert* had brought me, we were getting serious reputations of being the "*Sex Pistols* of Ufology," while our then-editor, Patrick Huyghe, played the role of Pistols' manager, Malcolm McClaren. But that was fine with both of us.

On the Friday night, a cocktail-party was held in Lisa's luxurious suite. Greg brought his girlfriend, Sigrid, along and everyone was soon tucking into the plentiful supply of food and drink that Lisa had thoughtfully provided for one and all. Jim Moseley wandered over, whisky and coke in hand, and we had a genial chat about beer, food, and just about everything and anything, aside from UFOs.

Lisa then had an idea: Why doesn't everyone say what he or she is thankful for? And so the collective throng all stood in a circle. Some people were thankful that Lisa, and people like her were putting on such events (and I think everyone agreed with that). Others were thankful that the UFO community was still digging deep as it sought to uncover the truth about UFOs that always seemed to tantalizingly elude us. The alcohol prevents me from recalling what I was thankful for, but whatever it was, it must have meant an awful lot to me at the time.

Then someone said that he was thankful for Colonel Philip Corso, author of a highly controversial and pro-UFO book on Roswell. As some people clapped loudly and others nodded earnestly, a disgusted and amazed Jim Moseley cried at the top of his voice: "Why?" Greg almost fell over with laughter, but others looked in his and Jim's direction with distinct disapproval. Whatever happened during the rest of the evening, I have no recollection of it, aside from the fact that around 2 a.m. the party ended, people staggered back to their respective rooms, and a new day beckoned.

On the Saturday morning, I was surprised to find that in addition to bringing Sigrid to the gig, Greg had brought someone else, too. That someone else was a smiling, long-haired character in a t-shirt who looked similar to any normal punter at such an event. But that was not the case. This character was none other than Walter Bosley. In the years before t-shirts and long hair were all-dominating for him, as Greg had noted, Walter Bosley was known by another title: Special Agent Walter Bosley—of the Air Force Office of Special Investigations, no less.

According to Greg, Bosley "was assigned to counterintelligence duties with two detachments of the AFOSI from 1994 to 1999. He says his office was proudest of the fact that for years, UFO stories (among others) were part of a program to keep various stealth technology projects under wraps, and usher any meddling inquiries behind the laughter curtain."

And as Bosley had noted to Greg: "I also initiated an investigation to look at hostile intelligence services and their use of unwitting U.S. citizens to collect info on defense technology. We went to a few UFO events around Southern California to check this kind of thing out." Precisely what the attendees at the NUFOC gig would have thought had they only known that an "evil government man" was secretly among them scarcely bears thinking about. Indeed, images of lynch mobs and out-of-control vigilantes wildly baying for blood sprung into my amused mind.

On Saturday afternoon, I took a stroll outside and checked out the Hollywood Walk of Fame that was only minutes away from the hotel. I told Dana, by phone, later that day that I had taken some pictures of one of the cemented stars.

"Whose did you get?" asked Dana, "Madonna? Tom Cruise?"

"Not exactly," I replied. "I got Godzilla's."

There was a moment of silence, followed by: "That big lizard thing, you mean?"

"Yeah, that's him."

"Baby!" she replied, in laughing exasperation, adding: "Only you could go to Hollywood and be surrounded by all those famous people, and all you want is Godzilla's star."

"Well, he's the greatest cryptozoological creation of cinema," I replied, quite seriously. "I can get some two-bit actor's star any time."

After that, it was time for a quick TV shoot with a team from the History Channel, who were there making a documentary on the Bermuda Triangle, and then it was back to the lecture theater, where I ran into alien abductee Melinda Leslie.

"Poor, Nick," she commiserated. "How could you get taken in by those disinformation people who told you that there were no aliens at Roswell?" It was a typical statement of the type that came regularly from those who desperately wanted to believe that beings from another galaxy had slammed into the desert floor at Roswell all those decades previously. I smiled, went on my way, and promptly ran into "Underground Base" researcher Richard Sauder, who similarly asserted that I had been blatantly lied to by my Roswell sources. I smiled again.

Then, only moments later, I was accosted by a wild-eyed figure who was so paranoid that surely not even the writers of *The X-Files* would have had anything to do with him. Did I know, he asked me earnestly, that "many people here" were having nosebleeds and had weird "implant marks on their necks?" No, I replied, I did not know that. He nodded slowly and grimly. I thanked him for his revelations, promised that I would let him know if I came across anyone who had been replaced by an alien clone, and headed for the bar. It couldn't be true, could it? Well, of course it couldn't. But it was *exactly* what people were saying when I met Dana at Laughlin in 2001. There was only one thing I knew for certain: It was truly time for a large, cold beer.

Later that evening, and after the day's lectures were over, there was a superb gala dinner, at which Jim Moseley gave a talk, that was packed with entertaining tale-after-entertaining tale about his more-than-half- century of involvement in the UFO subject. And it would not be a Jim Moseley lecture without a mention of the classic story of UFO author Gray Barker's typewriter that now resides deeply cemented in a wall somewhere, and well out of the hands of the government agents who a paranoid Barker thought (possibly with very good reason) were hot on his, and the typewriter's, trail. Jim tells the story far better than I ever could; and if you are not acquainted with this strange saga, I recommend you secure a copy of his book *Shockingly Close to the Truth*—shocking because it was written with a former CIA man and UFO writer named Karl Pflock, for the full and unexpurgated facts.

It was at around 8 a.m. on the Sunday morning when I delivered my own lecture on *Body Snatchers in the Desert*, and I suspect that many people who were not exactly happy about the fact that I had dared to suggest anything other than an alien spacecraft had crashed at Roswell on that fateful day in 1947, were secretly pleased and relieved that very few people would be up and alert at that unearthly hour to hear my demolition job. Hell, after a night of revelry I can hardly say that I was alert—and I was the speaker. Nevertheless, a reasonably sized audience did turn up, including Jim Castle and Scott Willman, two influential figures in the world of Los Angeles television, who were then casting for a new reality show on the paranormal. When, after my lecture was finished, they approached me and asked if I would be interested in taking part in the show, I—never one to turn down the opportunity to promote my research—said yes. I confess, however, that I doubted anything would develop from the invitation. I should have had more faith, however, as will later become apparent. But after concluding my lecture, I had other things on my mind.

Later on Sunday, I had to head to LAX Airport for a flight back to Dallas, and so I said my goodbyes to Greg, and to the rest of the crowd, and jumped into a cab. The nighttime flight to Dallas was a quiet one, with barely 30 seats taken on the all-but-empty aircraft. I had taken with me to the NUFOC conference a case full of second-hand books, most of which I had sold at the event, and that had resulted in me having a pocket stuffed to the bursting point with dollar bills. As we prepared for take-off I told one of the flight attendants that if she needed change, she could give me a 20-dollar bill, and in return I would give her 20 one-dollar bills. She was delighted by this and a deal was struck. It was a deal that provided me with a plentiful supply of free wine for the duration of the entire flight in return for my financial help. And so I settled down with one of my all-time favorite books, Jack Kerouac's *Big Sur*, and heartily enjoyed my ever-flowing free drinks and endless packets of peanuts.

I couldn't relax too much though. I was due to get back to Dallas around midnight. Then I had a 45 minute drive back home. But that was not all: at 6 a.m. on the following morning I had to be back at Dallas-Fort Worth International Airport. I was on my way to Puerto Rico again for a week. My quarry: the monstrous Chupacabras, of course.

15

Back to the Island of Blood

Having already included within the pages of this book a chapter on my 2004 expedition to Puerto Rico with Jon Downes and the Sci Fi Channel's *Proof Positive* team, I would have happily avoided chronicling the details of my September 2005 trip. However, the second excursion revealed such a wealth of new and startling data on the bloodsucker of the island that I simply cannot omit or resist a deep discussion of the events in question.

It was late one night in the early summer of 2005 when Canadian filmmaker Paul Kimball, of Red Star Films, and with whom I had worked on a number of earlier projects, phoned me with a proposition. His company, Paul explained, had just been commissioned by Canada's Space Channel to make a documentary titled *Fields of Fear*, the subject of which would be animal mutilations in the United States, Canada, and Puerto Rico. Paul knew that I had been to the island previously, that I had established good contacts and leads there, and that I had written about official, FBI files on animal mutilations in my 2003 book, *Strange Secrets: Real Government Files on the Unknown.* As a result, Paul hired me as both a consultant to, and a participant in, the show. And so it was that barely hours after getting back home from the NUFOC gig, I was airborne once again for the island of mystery.

Paul, in an earnest, and presumably successful, effort to save a fistful of dollars, had me on a bizarre flight path. In 2004, the Sci Fi Channel had me flying on a sensible, direct journey from Texas to Florida, and finally on to Puerto Rico. But that was not good enough for Paul. He apparently spent hours tirelessly burning the midnight oil and surfing the Internet to find the very best deal possible. The result was a money-saving flight that took me from Dallas to Puerto Rico via, of all places, Chicago! But it was a journey that would not be without its curiosities.

As we sat on the tarmac, waiting for the Puerto Rico-bound plane to take off from Chicago's airport, I got chatting with the guy who sat next to me. It transpired that he served with the U.S. Army, and had a fiancée on the island, whom he was going to visit. They were due to marry in 2006. Bob was his name and, after I told him of my reasons for traveling to Puerto Rico, we got into a brief, but deep and entertaining, discussion about all things paranormal and mysterious. Bob told me that he had heard all sorts of odd stories on the island about the Chupacabras, about aliens, and about underground bases. He then asked me about my opinions on Roswell.

I told him that, in my view, Roswell had more to do with diabolical human experimentation than it did with aliens, and he listened intently. The always slightly paranoid part of me wondered if he was, perhaps, listening too intently, and the reason why he, a military man, conveniently sat next to me was to pump me for information. I made sure he never had the opportunity to surreptitiously drop anything of a deadly nature into my drink.

We were still on the runway when Bob asked me: "Wasn't there a secret group that supposedly hid the Roswell story? And didn't some files supposedly surface from them a few years back?"

"Yeah," I replied. "It was called MJ12, which was supposed to be this group of high-flyers in the government and the military who were keeping it all under wraps. But I think that the files were disinformation to hide the human experiment angle." I added: "The MJ12 researchers have got it all back-to-front."

No lie: At the exact moment I uttered those words, an aircraft passed us slowly on an adjoining runway, and, out of the window, I could see that its tail-numbers ended: 12MJ. I stared, just utterly startled. 12MJ: MJ12 back-to-front. The gods of synchronicity were certainly playing strange mind-games with me that day. Bob smiled intently, and in a distinctly sinister fashion in my direction, as I pointed out the odd coincidence at work. I carefully moved my drink yet further out of his way to ensure that nothing of a chemical or biological nature made its way into the bottle. Only minutes after take-off, however, Bob was sound asleep and he barely moved until landing. I settled back into my seat with my well-worn copy of Hunter S. Thompson's *The Rum Diary*, a whisky and Coke, and a pleasant chicken dinner for company.

Darkness had enveloped Puerto Rico by the time we closed in on the island, and the flickering lights of the city of San Juan, and the silhouetted hills of the El Yunque rainforest, made for a glorious view out of the window. It was a view that I relished and absorbed for as long as I possibly could. Then we were on the ground. I said my goodbyes to a bleary-eyed Bob the soldier, collected my case from baggage claim, and there was Paul waiting for me, along with his brother Jim, and the film crew: John Rosborough and Findlay Muir. Findlay was a Scot by birth, and had lived in Canada for years, but he still retained enough of his Scottish accent to allow me to instantly recognize where he was from. I knew Jim and John already, having met them both with Paul at the Aztec, New Mexico, "crashed UFO" conference in early 2003. Greetings exchanged, we headed for the hotel and then dinner.

Over our meals, Paul explained to me that he had hired the services of a local "Chupacabras expert" named Orlando Pla, who I would get to meet the next day. Orlando was going to act as our guide, and had arranged a wealth of interviews for us at a multitude of locations. And so, the three Canadians, the Scotsman, and the Englishman (all of whom were transplanted to the United States), sat in the Puerto Rican restaurant, intently discussing vampires for the next two hours.

Paul, to my joy, was not one of those annoyingly intense film producer-directors who was a slave to his art, and who had to be up at the crack of dawn every day. So, we wisely agreed to meet each morning in the hotel lobby at the far more sensible hour of around 9 a.m. Thus, after leaving the restaurant, and in no rush to grab some sleep, Paul and I strolled around the hotel and then sat chatting outside for a while, watching tiny crabs running wildly around the hotel's gardens that backed onto the ocean.

As waves crashed violently against the rocks, I casually informed Paul that when I was on the island in the previous year with Jon Downes, we were told to carefully avoid coming into contact with the local bat population—unless we wanted to risk contracting rabies. Paul looked genuinely worried and asked if I thought it would be possible to film the entire show from the safe confines of the hotel. I told him, no, it would not. I wasn't entirely sure that he was joking, either. We then headed to the hotel's casino where Paul won $1.50. "Now I can put that toward your airfare," he told me, with a broad, beaming smile on his face that almost took on maniacal proportions. Again, I wasn't sure he was entirely joking.

After a breakfast of fruit and hot tea, I met with the other guys, who had entirely taken over the lobby with camera gear, sound equipment, and a host of other items of a technical nature. A slightly stressed-out and frowning Jim was busily trying to get everything loaded into the minivan that they had rented for the week, and was working to keep everything running on schedule. I could see a big, dark-haired guy of middle age talking to Paul, and I figured that it had to be Orlando. It was. Paul introduced me to him, and we got to chatting. It transpired that Orlando had been investigating the paranormal mysteries of Puerto Rico for years, and was an absolute fountain of knowledge on everything from the Chupacabras to UFOs, from Bigfoot to ghosts, and more. Finally, the vehicle was fully loaded and we all climbed aboard. For some reason, we kept the same seats all week: Jim was driving and Orlando sat next to him. I was directly behind Jim, Paul was to my right, and John and Findlay were in the back with the gear. Snacks and drinks were purchased, and on what promised to be a blisteringly hot day, we headed off into the unknown.

"The Chupacabras is a marketing name for a phenomenon," said Orlando, as Jim carefully negotiated the bustling streets of San Juan. Orlando explained to us that the island was home to a whole range of mysteries that had become lumped under the Chupacabras banner, and they might not actually all be connected. I asked Orlando what he meant by this, and he replied that there were several strange things going on. Firstly, there were reports of diabolical and dangerous creatures seen deep within El Yunque that, Orlando elaborated, sounded eerily like the deadly Raptors from *Jurassic Park*.

"This is a fearsome beast that walks on two legs and is supposed to be a large reptile," Orlando added.

"That would be cool if we got to film one of those," I said to Paul, who was somewhat skeptical of the whole affair, and merely nodded with a look of amusement and bemusement on his face. Within minutes we had left the concrete of San Juan behind us and we were heading down the highway for the forests. As we drove, Orlando told us the amusing story of a woman named Mildred, who claimed to have seen, on numerous occasions, UFOs landing at San Juan Airport several years before. The UFOs, said Mildred, were coming from the United States and Canada and ingeniously disguised themselves as United Airlines passenger jets to avoid detection. We all laughed at that one.

"Do you know what you should do if you see a Chupacabras?" asked Orlando, matter-of-factly. We all shook our heads. "Well," he added, "legend says that if you see the spikes go up on its back you should sing it a song, a lullaby, which will calm it, and then you should run as fast as you can." Paul said he would forget the lullaby and just run. I thought Orlando would be a full-on believer in the idea that the Chupacabras and the associated animal mutilations were connected, but he was not. Indeed, he spent as much time telling us as many of the unbelievable tales he had come across as those that seemed genuine.

But what fascinated me most of all was Orlando's theory that the Chupacabras was some form of "social experiment" created by the United States Government to: (a) try and understand how people might react to the presence of extraterrestrials; (b) utilize as a convenient cover to hide dark and dubious things that the Army was secretly doing on the island; and (c) determine how rumors spread, and the way in which those same rumors could be controlled and manipulated for psychological warfare purposes.

As far as the grisly mutilations and deaths of animals on the island were concerned, Orlando said firmly and concisely: "We must first point the finger at the U.S. Government." As we continued on our drive and the scenery grew wilder and greener, Orlando mentioned that stories had been quietly circulating among the island's inhabitants for years to the effect that there were some distinctly strange things going on in the rainforest at a U.S. Air Force "Primate Research Center." So the story went, biological warfare tests, genetic manipulation, and more was the order of the day, and some of the unfortunate animals that had been experimented on had escaped from their confines and were running wild on the island. At least some of those animals, it was suspected, could have been responsible for the tales of the Chupacabras's exploits.

This was a theory that Jon Downes and I had come face to face with the previous year, and that Jon had told me was extremely prevalent when he was there in 1998, too. Similarly, in my book *Strange Secrets* I had revealed how American psychological warfare planners in the 1950s had spread tales of blood-sucking vampires in the Philippines to spook superstitious, enemy rebels. It did not take long for me to learn that there was a lot of distrust in Puerto Rico about the American military presence; and, inevitably, tales such as this about the Chupacabras being the result of Frankenstein-like experimentation undertaken by evil government people proliferated. Notably, the story claimed that the CIA was also linked with this research center, and Agency interest was focused specifically upon "social behavior studies," related to monkey experimentation and Chupacabras attacks.

None of us truly believed that even the best scientists of the United States Government had the skills to mutate a friendly little monkey into a rampaging, blood-sucking killing-machine with glowing eyes, razor-sharp claws, and vicious-looking spikes running down the length of its back. But there was no doubt that bizarre things of a genetic nature were afoot deep in the forest. Such a "Primate Research Center" most assuredly did exist. In fact, several years earlier, a number of monkeys had escaped from the center, and were now running wildly and breeding in the woods. But most disturbing was the fact that the original escapees had been used in experiments to try and find a cure for AIDS. In other words, HIV-infected monkeys were on the loose in Puerto Rico, and in the exact areas in which we would be trekking. It was highly possible, Orlando theorized, that some attacks attributed to Puerto Rico's most famous vampire were really the result of the predations of a "very aggressive monkey" that had escaped from such a laboratory. And arguably, he added, that would be a very good reason for the U.S. Government to create tales about the Chupacabras: It would act as good camouflage in the event of any truly horrific attacks on local livestock, or worse still, on people.

"My God," said Paul loudly, "There's a Chupacabras, rabies-infected bats, and now wild monkeys with AIDS! What next?" It was a good question. And as Orlando told us, there was plenty more to come. I'm not entirely sure that pleased Paul, however. There was, for example, the story told by Orlando of Feredo, a private detective who had been contracted by the FBI to investigate devil-worshipping cults on the island. As Orlando stated starkly: "Puerto Rico has Voodoo and Black Magic."

During the course of his investigations, Feredo had come across a number of reports of animal attacks that had been attributed to the Chupacabras, and where the animals had the classic two-puncture wounds on the neck and bodies utterly drained of blood. Interestingly, however, in some cases where the victims had been punctured, it looked suspiciously, as though someone had carefully shaved away the surrounding hair. I was quite open to the idea that the Chupacabras was a real beast of unknown origins. But I most definitely could not believe that the beast carried a razor and shaving cream with it as it merrily slaughtered the wildlife of Puerto Rico. Again, this suggested that psychological manipulation was at work, and that at least some stories of Chupacabras attacks might have been generated by devil cults who were using the mystery as a highly convenient cover for their own nefarious bloodletting rites.

Orlando was about to tell us more when Jim said that we were about to arrive at our first location.

We turned off the main road and headed up an incredibly steep hill that was surrounded by thick, overhanging trees and bushes, and I actually wondered if the vehicle would make the climb. But it did—just about—and we came to a halt at the top of the hill, several hundred feet above the highway, and that afforded us a truly incredible view of the surrounding prehistoric-looking countryside. Findlay off-loaded the equipment and John fixed microphones to Orlando and me. The plan was to have me as the expedition's roving reporter, with Orlando as the man that would lead me on my quest for the truth about all things bloodsucking and vampire-like.

One of the things that Orlando thought would be good to discuss was the activity at a former U.S. Naval base called Roosevelt Roads, which we could see a mile or so from us. The U.S. Navy had closed down the base on March 31, 2004, which was seen as a victory for the progressive and pro-independence forces of the island, coming as it did shortly after the people of Puerto Rico had also won the fight to stop the U.S. Navy's use of the island municipality of Vieques for bombing practice. The Navy had been forced to close down Camp García, the firing zone in Vieques, on May 1, 2003 after using the area for target practice since the 1940s.

According to the story that Orlando relayed, a number of captured, and very vicious, Chupacabras had supposedly been held at Roosevelt Roads at some point in the 1990s. The story was that they had been secretly shipped to the States—probably to Area 51 or some such similar desert locale. The story was a great one, but it sounded similar to classic folklore, and very similar to the tales told about alien bodies held in cryogenic storage in the cavernous bowels of Wright-Patterson Air Force Base's mythical *Hangar 18*. Nevertheless, it was an integral part of the Chupacabras controversy, and so discuss it we most assuredly did.

Orlando pointed in the direction of the base for the benefit of the cameras, and I nodded earnestly as we began a discussion of what had, or had not happened, and mused upon the tales of caged beasts of unknown origin held by the Navy. Whatever the truth of the affair, the interview definitely made for good TV; and Paul, after all that worry about AIDS and rabies, was now a happy man.

With the first interview out of the way, we climbed aboard the van and headed off for destination number two. Again, Orlando was full of stories. There were the various U.S. Army whistleblowers that had told him tales of "radiation experiments" undertaken in the rainforest, of military pilots flying black-colored hang-gliders high over El Yunque late at night on spying missions and dope-drops, and of ecological tests of a strange and disturbing nature. And once more, there was the theory that this was all somehow connected with concocted tales of the Chupacabras that were circulated by officials to hide far more down to earth and controversial activities. But the real highlight of the day, for me at least, would come after lunch.

Orlando had arranged for us to interview a man named Miguel, a Shaman who devotedly cared for a sacred place on Puerto Rico know as the Town of the Stones. This was an incredibly spiritual location where one could commune with Earth-spirits, become one with Nature, and generally have an uplifting experience with the gods of old. Walking into the Town of the Stones, which was hidden behind a mass of trees and a gated pathway, was not unlike discovering a hidden grotto in the middle of New York. Small caves, winding pathways, and a circle of standing stones dominated the area, and a feeling of magic and tranquility filled the air.

As the interview with Miguel progressed, we learned that back in the 1990s he had worked for Puerto Rico's Civil Defense people, and had officially investigated numerous Chupacabras attacks for the government. Indeed, at one point Miguel stuck his hand through the open window of his truck and pulled out a thick, bound folder that was crammed with newspaper articles, reports, drawings, and paintings of the Chupacabras, all of which he had faithfully collected and collated during his time as an official investigator of the mystery. It was a veritable *Treasure Island* of data of the type that I had never come across before, and told a unique story of the beast, the witnesses, and the response of the Civil Defense personnel. Miguel had no doubt that the Chupacabras existed, but from where it came, he had no real idea.

Of one thing Miguel *was* certain, however: The creature was highly dangerous. He displayed for us numerous photographs of animals, predominantly cattle and goats, that had been attacked and violently mutilated by the Chupacabras. He also showed us artistic renditions of the vicious spikes that reportedly ran down its back. The interview was soon completed, we thanked Miguel, and, with the day's activities now over, headed back to San Juan.

That evening, we met in the bar for an evening of food and revelry, and discussed the day's events and what was planned for tomorrow. Orlando, Paul said, had lined up yet another interview with a source from the Civil Defense group. In addition, we would be visiting a farmer who had received a visit from the mysterious Men in Black after one of his animals had been attacked by the beast.

"Life's never dull in this game, is it?" I asked Paul, in what was really a statement rather than a question. He heartily agreed. We toasted to a continued, productive week, and thanked God that we didn't have to work in the real world of 9-to-5. The conversation then turned to music, beer, gambling, and more, and bloodsucking vampires were forgotten about for the rest of the night. We headed back to our rooms around the witching hour, and morning soon arrived.

Once again, we met, with military precision, in the lobby at 9 a.m. sharp, and headed to the offices of Wisbel Alaya, a prime mover in Civil Defense who had been at the forefront of Chupacabras investigations a decade earlier. Alaya's offices were situated in a small, red-and-white concrete building in a pleasant little town some distance from San Juan, and he and his staff made us feel very welcome as we sat and chatted about the notoriety surrounding the Chupacabras. Whereas Miguel the Shaman was convinced that the files of the Civil Defense investigators demonstrated that something truly strange, perhaps even supernatural, was afoot on Puerto Rico, Wisbel took a very different view.

He was quite happy to be filmed, and told us how his team had sent blood, DNA, and skin samples taken from alleged victims of the Chupacabras to university professors, to forensic laboratories, and to just about anyone and everyone who might be able to offer an informed opinion on what it was that was taking place. Wisbel was certain that many of the stories were simply the collective result of unbridled paranoia, superstition, and an ever-churning rumor mill. Those cases where genuine killings and mutilations had occurred, he said, were the work of dogs, both wild and domestic. Even though many armchair believers might be inclined to disagree with Wisbel, he *had* investigated such cases firsthand, and they had not. But the fact that Miguel the Shaman worked for the same people, but had come to a completely different conclusion, demonstrated perfectly the way in which wildly differing opinions were formed regarding the nature of the beast.

After saying our goodbyes to Wisbel and his team, the weather began to turn bad. What had begun as a blisteringly hot day, rapidly turned into a deluge of biblical proportions, as El Yunque became nothing more than a blurry haze amid the rain-sodden clouds that hung low and ominously in the sky line. So, with filming well and truly halted for a while, we sat around chatting in a local eatery where I had a tuna salad that would present problems later on when I was hit by a spectacular bout of Montezuma's Revenge. But that is a story that I will not inflict upon those of a delicate disposition. Instead, I will share with you another story from Orlando, who had heard the highly intriguing tale that various druglords on the island were using the UFO subject as a cover for "marijuana drops" on the island.

There was no doubt that Puerto Rico was full to the brim with tales of strange lights seen over El Yunque late at night and in the early house of the morning. And while some of them *could* have been UFOs, I thought it far more plausible that the UFO theories were created at an official level to hide something exactly like illegal drug operations, perhaps using unmarked helicopters or even hang gliders of the type that Orlando had told us were being seen on occasion. But that conversation was curtailed when the weather began to improve and we headed for our next port of call.

Investigating a case that linked the dreaded Men in Black with the Chupacabras intrigued me greatly, and I was not disappointed by the way in which the afternoon developed. Antonio was a pig farmer whose small property was about a 30-minute drive from where we had parked during the storm. In 2000, one of his animals had been killed, after darkness had fallen, by the now familiar puncture marks to the neck. In this case, however, the animal exhibited three such marks, rather than the usual two. In addition, a number of rabbits kept on the property had been slaughtered in identical fashion.

At the time that all of the carnage was taking place, a considerable commotion was, quite naturally, being made by the animals. As a result, Antonio had rushed wildly out of his house with a machete in his hand, and had flung it in the direction of the marauding predator. Oddly, he told us that the machete seemed to bounce off something that seemed distinctly metallic in nature. In fact, Antonio suggested that what the machete had made contact with was armor-plated. Due to the overwhelming darkness, he had no idea what it was, however. But something was prowling around the property. The machete was later given to Antonio's cousin for safekeeping. The oddest aspect of the affair was still to come, however.

Shortly after the killing of the pig and the rabbits, a man and woman, dressed entirely in black, no less, descended on the farm and asked Antonio a wealth of questions about what had occurred, what he had seen, and the way in which his animals had met their grisly fates. Antonio was not threatened, he told us, but he had no doubt that someone at an official level was highly interested in determining what had take place. The pair thanked the bemused farmer, in a somewhat emotionless fashion, and left without uttering another word.

One thing that Antonio told us he had held back from his two mysterious visitors was that, on the morning after the attack, he had found strange footprints on his property that were spread quite a distance from each other, and he formed the opinion that whatever made them had the ability to leap considerable distances, in a fashion similar to that of a kangaroo. Leaping monsters, Men (and women) in Black, and mutilated animals collectively suggested that even if some of the tales of the Chupacabras were the creation of psychological warfare operatives, not all of them could be said to fall into such a category. There did appear to be something deadly lurking in the forest. And with another aspect of the quest completed, it was back to the hotel.

That night, me, Paul, John, and Findlay had dinner in an Italian restaurant that was situated within the hotel. The food and wine were superb, and we sat around chatting for hours. John, it transpired, had a highly enviable job. Although he was a freelancer, John spent much of his time working on a show called *Sea Hunters* for the National Geographic Channel. And it was a show that saw John and his crew roaming around the world to exotic locations to film shows on shipwrecks that had entertaining historical stories attached to them. I told John that it sounded like a wonderful job, and he agreed, with a broad grin on his face. And it was a great way to meet women, too, he added. I did not doubt it. Findlay and I discussed life back in Britain, and how we had each acclimatized to our new environs across the Atlantic. It was a good night—aside from when the curse of Montezuma kicked in not long after.

By the next day I was relatively recovered from my bout with the tuna salad of the previous day. Once again, we were bound for El Yunque, and this was a trip that would subsequently result in a meeting of highly strange and unbelievable proportions. As we turned off the highway and onto a steep and winding road that led deep into the heart of the hills and the immense forest, I realized

The El Yunque Rain Forest of Puerto Rico, home to the blood-sucking Chupacabras.

that we were on one of the roads that I had taken with Jon Downes the previous year when we were filmed for the Sci Fi Channel. We headed for a large, stone tower, similar to what you would expect to see affixed to an old English castle, situated high in the forest, which required a walk up a flight of what seemed like 1,000 steps to reach its summit. John and Findlay set up the cameras, and I interviewed Orlando about the Chupacabras attacks that had occurred within the rainforest. Findlay was securing some stunning panoramic shots of a type that could only be obtained from the top of the immense tower when something odd happened.

There were several people milling around quietly at the top of the tower as we filmed. And when the shoot was over, a woman asked me: "Are you from Wolverhampton?" This was a reference to a bustling town about 6 miles from where I used to live in England. Amazed to hear a local accent, I said that, no, I wasn't from the town, but the picturesque English village I had lived in, Pelsall, was only a stone's throw away.

"Oh, yes, I know Pelsall," she replied, matter-of-factly, adding: "My cousin and her husband live there."

It would later transpire that my dad, who also lives in Pelsall, actually knew the husband of the woman's cousin, whose name was David Malpas, and who lived only a few streets away from my dad's house. Paul and Findlay looked on with incredulity as this coincidence of epic proportions played out. What were the chances, I wondered, of me bumping into someone, atop a remote tower deep in the heart of Puerto Rico's El Yunque rainforest on a November morning, whose cousin lived in the same village I had grown up in? As with the affair of the 12MJ-MJ12 tail-numbers on

Your fearless author finally comes face-to-face with the Chupacabras.

the aircraft in Chicago, the gods of synchronicity were still playing their strange games of manipulation.

And the synchronicities continued unabated. After a delicious lunch, we headed for a place of worship known as the Church of the Three Kings, which was a delightful old building that looked like a combination of a Medieval English castle and something you would see in a dusty Mexican town in one of those old spaghetti-westerns. But this was surrounded by dense, green woods on all sides rather than desert, and was topped off with a large, five-pointed star that reached out to the heavens from the church's flat roof. Our interviewee was a barrel-chested figure named Pucho who had an amazing tale to tell us.

As the crew set up the equipment, little kids, excitedly chattering, came running out of the woods to see what all of the fuss was about, and a teenager insisted on riding by at every moment on a noisy, rusty old motorbike that was definitely well past its prime. Pucho shouted something in the direction of the bike and the rider, looking hurt, vanished into the sunset, never to be seen again. Pucho then settled back, folded his arms, and proceeded to relate his story.

It was long after the sun had set on a weeknight in February 2005, and Pucho was walking past the Church of the Three Kings when he heard what he described as a "loud roar" coming from a particularly dense section of trees adjacent to the building. And as Pucho explained, he was amazed to see a huge, feathery bird come looming out of the tree canopy. Oddly, the bird did not merely fly out, but seemed to levitate vertically in the fashion of a helicopter, before it soared high into the air and headed off in the direction of a nearby farm. Stressing that he had never before or since seen such an immense beast, Pucho could only watch in stark terror and utter shock until the creature was out of sight. Notably, several days later the farm where the creature was seen flying towards suffered a number of horrifying attacks on its livestock.

But, what of the synchronicity that I mentioned? Well, you will recall that when I visited the island in 2004 with Jon Downes, we interviewed a woman named Norka, whose encounter with Puerto Rico's winged nightmare occurred in roughly the same time frame that encounters were taking place in England with a similar beast known as the Owlman.

What was interesting about the Owlman encounters was that they all occurred in the dark woods surrounding a place called Mawnan Old Church, which was situated in the ancient and folklore-dominated county of Cornwall. One of the witnesses to his Owliness (as the creature later became known), Jane Greenwood, described her encounter in the summer of 1976 to the *Falmouth Packet* newspaper, after a number of earlier reports had made the headlines:

"I am on holiday in Cornwall with my sister and our mother. I, too, have seen a big bird-thing. It was Sunday morning, and the place was in the trees near Mawnan Church, above the rocky beach. It was in the trees standing like a full-grown man, but the legs bent backwards like a bird's. It saw us, and quickly jumped up and rose straight up through the trees." And as young Jane perceptively asked: "How could it rise up like that?"

How, indeed? It was exactly that question that Pucho wanted an answer to 29 years later. Personally, I wanted to know what sort of creature it was that seemed to manifest in woods adjacent to ancient, sacred grounds on opposite sides of the world and decades apart, and where the witnesses described the movements of the animal in practically an identical fashion? It is a question I still ask myself—obsessed, as I am, with such diabolical weirdness.

Pucho was very matter-of-fact about the encounter, cared not a bit about publicity, and just wanted to know what was afoot in darkest Puerto Rico. We could not help him, beyond confirming that the island was a truly strange place; and whatever it was that he saw, it had no place roaming around the wilder parts of his homeland. He laughed loud as if to say: "*You* are telling *me*?" On that note, we said our farewells, took one last look at the scene of all the strangeness, just in case the beast decided to make a reappearance for the cameras, and began our hour-long journey back to the hotel.

Twenty-four hours later, we were sat on the driveway of a medium-sized house at the top of a large hill that afforded us a spectacular view of El Yunque. It was 6 p.m. and we were all starved, but there was work to be done. We had originally planned to do another interview that day, but an unfortunate fire led to the cancellation of that appointment. Luckily, the house owner kept us supplied with snacks and cokes; and, with Orlando translating, he told us how some of his pigs, that were housed in a ramshackle pen at the foot of a steep, winding and muddy pathway at the back of his home, had been attacked and mutilated. It was, by now, a familiar tale of carnage, massive blood loss, and of something devilishly disturbing prowling the countryside after sunset.

That night was our last one in Puerto Rico, and I had hoped that we would be hitting San Juan for a bit of partying. But it was not to be. Paul wanted to film some last-minute head-and-shoulder shots of me in his hotel room, summarizing the events of the bizarre week, and so that became the priority. We wrapped up around 11 p.m., and had a morning call at 5 a.m., so we opted to have a couple of hours at the hotel bar before retiring to our rooms and the pain-in-the-neck chore of packing.

My room was situated near a piece of ocean out of which a large, jagged piece of rock stood, pointing proudly outward and upward. Orlando had told me of an old legend tied to this particular piece of rock. So the tale went, centuries ago a fisherman had gone out to sea at that point and had never returned. The man's faithful hound had waited patiently at the shore for his master to come home, but it was never to be. Such was the dog's devotion, however, his long and lonely years-long vigil resulted in the animal being turned into a solid block of stone. Even though the tale was simply that, a tale, I felt a tinge of sadness as I looked over the balcony and saw the cold, harsh waves crash against the rock unrelentingly. But it was now 2 a.m., and I had to be in the lobby in four hours time, so I bid goodnight to the craggy canine, and hit the hay.

Everyone seemed to have completely different flight schedules back home, and as the only ones whose flights were around the same time as mine were Paul and Findlay, the three of us grabbed a cab, and said our farewells to the others. Sadly, I never got to say goodbye to Orlando, who had mysteriously vanished into the darkness the previous night before I had chance to utter even a single word in his direction.

On the flight home, I considered what we had learned. Whereas on my 2004 expedition with Jon Downes, I had come to the conclusion that we were dealing with one form of animal that had paranormal overtones to it, I was now convinced that there were other things afoot, too. From what Orlando had to say, at least, it seemed the mythology of the Chupacabras was being ingeniously manipulated by the U.S. Government as a part of its on-going animal experimentation, and by drug-dealers who were spreading tales of UFOs and fierce creatures as a way of keeping superstitious locals out of those areas of El Yunque where their operations were taking place.

In addition and again based on what Orlando told us, I would not be surprised if there were other, weird animals living deep in the rain forest that had probably led, in part at least, to the legend of the Chupacabras. But still, I *was* of the opinion that some form of unholy life form—and perhaps one from a realm of existence that was outside of our current understanding, given all of the odd synchronicities that seemed to bedevil us, and its ability to avoid capture—was lurking in the darker and wilder parts of Puerto Rico. It was a cunning and deadly predator, and whatever it was, it was not going away anytime soon. Yes, Puerto Rico was still a land of profound oddities. But, still, my journeying was not over.

16

The Never-Ending Journey

One week after Puerto Rico, I was Michigan-bound and specifically to Detroit, where Bill Konkolesky of the local Mutual UFO Network (MUFON) chapter had booked me to speak on my book *Body Snatchers in the Desert*. Present at the meeting was Lisa Shiel. I had met Lisa earlier in 2005 at the monthly meeting of the Dallas-Fort Worth MUFON group, and had written the Foreword to her book *Backyard Bigfoot* that was her own, personal study of Bigfoot activity in the state of Texas—including encounters on her own property, which is situated within a heavily wooded area outside of Fort Worth.

I was surprised to see Lisa at the Detroit meeting, and she explained that she had recently relocated there from the Lone Star

State. And the hairy entities of the Texas woods had apparently followed her. Lisa relayed to me how she was seeing exactly the same type of activity near her rural Michigan home that she had uncovered in Texas. Again, this was evidence to me that whatever these hairy entities really were, they enjoyed playing bizarre mind games with the people that investigated them. I then had a few weeks at home with Dana before the road beckoned once again—to Roswell.

I mentioned earlier how, at the NUFOC gig in Hollywood in August 2005, I had met with TV producers Scott Willman and Jim Castle. Scott had an impressive pedigree, and Jim had worked on numerous episodes of *The X-Files*. But they had a new and exciting project to get their collective teeth into now. The idea was to create a show that was part reality TV and part *X-Files*, which would revolve around a team of paranormal experts traveling the world in search of the unexplained. Was I interested in being a part of that team, Jim and Scott asked? I was. And so it was on a Sunday morning in mid-November 2005 that we filmed a pilot episode based around what is arguably the biggest draw in conspiracy fields: Roswell.

The company had come up with a huge budget and the filming took place at the former Norton Air Force Base in San Bernardino, California, and within the town of Roswell itself. So, in mid-November 2005 I took a flight from Amarillo (where Dana and I temporarily relocated to in early November to help take care of her grandmother who was recovering from major surgery) for yet another excursion into the unknown.

In addition to me, the team was comprised of well-known paranormal investigator and author Josh Warren, his buddy Brian Irish, UFO hunter Ruben Uriarte, psychics Laura Lee and Karyn Reece, unsolved mystery author Heidi Hollis, Native American Indian Richard Hernandez, and best-selling author Jim Marrs. On arriving at the old air base (that now falls under the jurisdiction of San Bernardino), all of us were impressed by the sheer amount of work and planning that had gone into the show; we were each provided with clothing: including t-shirts (unfortunately not black), sweatshirts, jackets, caps, watches, and even three brand new, all-terrain vehicles.

And when we arrived at Norton, we were all amazed at the scene before us: a large studio had been built in one of the huge hangars that had been converted into a kind of forensic laboratory. Alien dummies were strewn across recreations of Army crates and gurneys, Bigfoot foot-casts were displayed on shelves, TV and computer screens flashed imagery of a multitude of unexplained phenomena, and countless photographs of ghosts, lake monsters, and much more adorned the walls of our lab. Interestingly, it was this same hangar that was utilized by the Sci Fi Channel to shoot scenes for Steven Spielberg's *Taken* series.

The premise of the pilot-show was an interesting and unique one: since no conventional route of investigation had completely resolved the Roswell enigma to everyone's satisfaction, why not employ the use of psychics to try and unravel the mystery? As a result, we flew to Roswell and actually undertook a midnight séance in Hangar 84 of the old Air Base, where it was alleged the bodies found at the crash site back in 1947 had been taken. The purpose: To try and psychically contact the souls of the Roswell entities—whatever their true point of origin—and question them with regard to what really did, or did not, happen on that fateful day 60 years ago.

But I'm getting slightly ahead of myself here. The filming began on Monday morning, with each of us giving head-and-shoulder-style interviews about our work and own areas of expertise. That was followed by dinner and a night on the town, another day

Roswell's famous UFO Museum.

of filming at San Bernardino, and then the flight to Roswell. Our first port of call in Roswell was the old base hospital where, even today, the nurses told us, they had seen little, black-eyed, spectral creatures roaming the corridors when darkness had fallen. Until 4 a.m. we stalked the ghostly Roswell entities, but they failed to put in an appearance.

The next day, we were bound for the town's Roswell UFO Museum, which had also been the site of ghostly activity. Lights would flash on and off, strange shadowy figures would lurk in the darkness, and from time to time an atmosphere of menace would descend on the old building. Of course, all of this made for excellent television as Josh Warren displayed his impressive array of electronic ghost-hunting equipment for the cameras, particularly when Josh, one of the nation's most respected and careful investigators, succeeded in detecting a wide range of anomalous phenomena that impressed everyone.

Friday was the busiest day of all. The morning began with a trip out to one of the alleged UFO crash sites. I say *one* of the sites because numerous locations have been offered where bodies and strange wreckage were supposedly found back in 1947. And so, our convoy of vehicles hit the road and headed out into the wilds of the desert, which was fine, that is until someone realized after we had got out there that no one had thought to bring any water. Some of the team had visions of us dying of dehydration at the site and, ironically, becoming the next victims of the Roswell crash. But we survived, and the film crew got some great footage of us roaming the site where, *maybe*, aliens from another world bit the dust six decades ago.

I apologize if it sounds like I'm racing through this, but I want to cut to the midnight séance in the old hangar back at Roswell, where some distinctly strange things of a truly monstrous nature occurred at the witching hour on that cold, bleak Friday night. It was a very weird experience, to say the least. I kid you not when I say that the temperature was freezing outside—and inside the hangar, too.

The crew set up, someone shouted "Action!" and we all duly entered the hangar and took our seats at a table, atop of which was a multitude of large candles. Karyn began to try to summon the long dead of Roswell. And the dead just may have come, too. The wind began to howl, and the walls of the hangar creaked and groaned loudly. At times, it sounded like footsteps were padding across the hangar roof above us, and an air of high strangeness overtook the team and crew. Even more so, when one of the cameramen said that he didn't feel well and promptly collapsed onto the floor. What had begun as an intriguing exercise was becoming something far darker.

But what was undoubtedly the creepiest, albeit, exciting, aspect of the night's activities was a startling piece of imagery captured, night-vision-style, by the camera team: namely nothing less than a spectral, snake-like entity that seemed to coil around the team as we sat at the table, holding hands and deep in meditation as we tried to summon up Roswell's dead. Indeed, a study of the film footage showed a brief image of what looked like a monstrous life-form that had been conjured up out of a diabolical, Lovecraftian nightmare. The slithering menace positively oozed uneasiness and dread; yet, seemingly was not intent on causing us harm, and vanished into the darkness above our table. And then it was all over; the dark atmosphere seemed to lift, and Jim Castle shouted: "It's a wrap." It was, and we headed back to the hotel, completely unaware at the time of what the cameras had recorded.

There is, however, no doubt in my mind that some form of contact was made on that dark, cold night in Hangar 84. Unfortunately, the show never aired, yet I am still hopeful that one day it will, and the mystery of Roswell and the ghostly secrets of Hangar 84 will finally be revealed to the world.

But far stranger, for me at least, was something that occurred after the filming was completed. After shooting for three days in Roswell, we returned to Norton Air Force Base to wrap up the program. And having done so, I decided to take a walk around the huge, empty base. I almost felt like I was immersed in an episode of *The X-Files*: Here I was wandering around an abandoned military facility, surrounded by discarded equipment, dusty old files that the military hadn't even bothered to remove from the battered old filing cabinets that still remained (for anyone who is interested, I pored over this Aladdin's Cave of material but found no smoking-guns), and an absolute maze of corridors, rooms, and underground entrance points that had undoubtedly once held secrets of who-knows-what proportions. But as I rounded one particular corner of one of the giant hangars I was amazed by the sight before me: a huge painting on the wall that depicted a futuristic spacecraft hovering over a craggy moon, while the planet Jupiter loomed in the background.

There was one, chief reason why this was of such interest to me. For years, it had been rumored that crashed alien technology had been secretly taken to Norton and had been "back-engineered" by American scientists. For example, in September 2000, it was revealed that a Lieutenant Colonel John Williams, who enlisted in the Air Force in 1964, had learned during the course of his career about a facility "inside of Norton Air Force Base in California that no one was to know about." The story was that "a UFO craft" was secretly being hidden within the bowels of the base. Similarly, Mark

McCandlish, an accomplished aerospace illustrator had gone on record as stating that a colleague of his (Brad Sorenson) had been inside a facility at Norton where he witnessed what were described as "alien reproduction vehicles" that were "fully functioning."

Although a private security company routinely toured the base, I quickly took a few photographs of the huge *Star Wars*-like painting for posterity. I have to say that seeing such advanced technology displayed in such a strange fashion did make me wonder about the nature of what had really gone on at Norton in years past. I scoured the base for a while longer—not really believing that I would find an actual, alien corpse, but you never know—and snapped more and more pictures. Most intriguing was one area of the floor in the main hangar that had been sealed with a thick layer of concrete. I mused—and still do—for a long time with regard to what secrets might still be hidden deep below Norton Air Force Base, in some dark, impenetrable vault. My search for a large hammer to smash my way into this underground realm was not successful. And so, with the rest of the crew I headed back to our San Bernardino hotel and a flight back to Amarillo.

The next few months were taken up with writing my book *Celebrity Secrets* and ghost-writing UFO researcher Bob Wood's first book for him: *In Search of the Alien Viruses*. But by April, the bulk of my work was done. As a self-employed writer, I always ensured that I had plenty of work to keep me busy, and this time was no different: I had a wealth of new projects that I wanted to immerse myself in. But it was time for a change: for five years we had been living in the United States; however, Dana had seen precious little of my home country. And so we decided to rectify that situation.

After finding love, adventure, and intrigue in the United States, and having chased, for five years, werewolves, Puerto Rican vampires, lake monsters, giant fish, gargoyles, Goat-Men, and more, we decided to head back to my home country of England for a while.

As word got out, offers to speak at conferences and other events in Britain surfaced; Jon Downes excitedly phoned me to tell me about a new wave of Sasquatch-type encounters that had just kicked-off in central England (which he practically begged me to investigate with him, and which, of course, I did), and Paul Kimball e-mailed to say that he wanted me on board for a new show he was filming in my native land. As we headed for Dallas-Fort Worth Airport and the transatlantic flight to the English city of Birmingham, Dana and I smiled at each other, and I reflected upon my half a decade in the States. Those five years had been immense fun and incredibly weird—which is just how I liked to live my life. I had no doubt that, whatever the future brought, trend was only set to continue.

And, indeed it did. But that, as they say, is a story for another day.

Resources

During the course of researching and writing this book, the following sources were consulted.

Chapter 1: The Story Begins

The UFO Congress: *www.ufocongress.com*

Chapter 2: Two Winged Things and a Wedding

Clark, Jerome, and Loren Coleman. *The Unidentified & Creatures of the Outer Edge: The Early Works of Jerome Clark and Loren Coleman.* Anomalist Books, 2006.

Chapter 3: Tales From Taos

A Visitors Guide to Northern New Mexico: *http://taoswebb.com*

Taos, New Mexico Vacation Guide: *www.taosvacationguide.com*

The Town of Taos: *www.taos.gov.com*

Chapter 4: Fangs, Fur, and Files

Godfrey, Linda S. *The Beast of Bray Road.* Prairie Oak Press, 2003.

Godfrey, Linda S. *Hunting the American Werewolf.* Trails Books, 2006.

Chapter 5: Monsters of the Big Thicket

The Big Thicket Directory of Southeast Texas: *www.bigthicketdirectory.com*

Big Thicket National Preserve: *www.nps.gov/bith*

Big Thicket National Preserve: *http://gorpaway.com/gorp/resource/us_national_park//tx_big_t.htm*

Handbook of Texas Online: *www.tsha.utexas.edu/handbook/online/articles/BB/gkb3.htm*

Ghost Road of Hardin County: *www.bigthicketdirectory.com*

The Bragg Road Ghost Lights: *www.qsl.net/w5www/bragg.html*

Briggs, Rob. *In the Big Thicket*. Paraview Press, 2001.

Sieveking, Paul. *Wild Things*. *Fortean Times*, 161.

Lopez, Barry. *Of Wolves and Men*. Touchstone Books, 1982.

Wild Woman of the Navidad: *www.texasescapes.com*

Dobie, J. Frank, ed. *The Legends of Texa*s. Texas Folklore Society, 1924.

The Wild Woman of the Navidad: *www.bigfootencounters.com/creatures/navidad.htm*

Bigfoot in Texas? *www.texasbigfoot.com/texbfhist1.html*

Chapter 6: A Menagerie of Monsters

The Annual UFO Crash Retrieval Conference: *www.ufoconference.com*

Godfrey, Linda. *Hunting the American Werewolf.* Trails Books, 2006.

Whitewater Rafting on the Upper Klamath River: *www.klamath-river.com*

Chapter 7: Spectral Animals

Warren, Joshua. *Pet Ghosts.* New Page Books, 2006.

Chapter 8: Creatures of the Black Lagoon

The Lady of the Lake: The Ghost of White Rock Lake: *www.watermelon-kid.com/places/wrl/lore/ghost.htm*

The Lady of White Rock Lake: *http://thefolklorist.com/horror/lakegirl.htm*

For the Love of the Lake: *www.whiterocklake.org/content/view/130/81/*

White Rock Lake Museum: *www.whiterocklakemuseum.org/index/htm*

White Rock Lake Foundation: *www.whiterocklakefoundation.org*

The Lady of the Lake Story: *www.whiterocklake.org/content/view/143/81/*

50 Reasons to Love (and Save) White Rock Lake, *D Magazine*, March 1995

The Rural Deities: *www.mythome.org/bfchxxii.html*

Dallas Morning News, September 7, 2002

Syers, Ed. *Ghost Stories of Texas.* Texian Press, 1981.

Farwell, Lisa. *Haunted Texas Vacations.* Westcliffe Publishers, 2000.

Chapter 9: In Search of Vampires

Primera Hora, December 3, 2004

In Search of Chupacabras. Nick Redfern, *Fate Magazine*, Vol. 58, No. 1, issue 657, 2005. See: *www.fatemag.com*

History of Puerto Rico: *http://welcome.topuertorico.org/history.shtml*

Puerto Rico History: *www.elyunque.com/history.html*

Puerto Rico History: *www.centropr.org*

History of Puerto Rico: *www.solboricua.com/history.htm*

Chapter 10: On the Track of Bigfoot

The Texas Bigfoot Research Center: *www.texasbigfoot.com*

Squatching: A Documentary: *www.squatching.com*

The Caddo Lake History Page: *www.caddolake.com/history.htm*

Caddo Lake, Texas-Louisiana: *http://ops.tamu.edu/x075bb/caddo/caddo.html*

Caddo Lake Area, Chamber of Commerce and Tourism: History: *http://caddolake.org/*

Man in Bigfoot Research, Scott Herriott:

http://txsasquatch.blogspot.com/2006/07/men-in-bigfoot-research-scott-herriott.html

Gulf Coast Bigfoot Research Organization: *www.gcbro.com*

Charlie DeVore Trusts His Nose, *Longview NewsJournal*, October 17, 2004

Chapter 11: Ghost Lights and Spooky Nights

History of Jefferson County, Texas: *www.co.jefferson.tx.us/historical_commission/hist.htm*

Ghost Stories: *http://historicjeffersonhotel.com/ghost.htm*

The Texas Ghost Lights Conference: *www.anomalyarchives.org/events 050611txghostlightsconf*

Chapter 12: Public Enemy Number One

Who's Who in UFOs and ETs: The Need for Discernment, (4th Edition), Nicholette Pavlevsky & Greg Wright, 2004

UFO Magazine, August/September, 2005

Chapter 13: The Goat-Man Cometh

Man or Beast? Goatman Lore Reborn in Fort Worth, Dallas Morning News, October 21, 1999

Fishy Man-Goat Terrifies Couples Parked at Lake Worth, Fort Worth Star-Telegram, July 10, 1969

Weird Texas, Wesley Treat, Heather Shade & Rob Riggs, Sterling Publishing Co., Inc., 2005

Bigfoot in Texas?: *www.bigfootproject.org/articles/bf_in_texas.html*

Chapter 14: Around the World in 30 Days

The National UFO Conference: *www.nufoc.org*

Project Beta, Greg Bishop, Paraview-Pocket Books, 2005

Shockingly Close to the Truth, James W. Moseley & Karl T. Pflock, Prometheus Books, 2002

Chapter 15: Back to the Island of Blood

History of Puerto Rico: *http://welcome.topuertorico.org/history.shtml*

Puerto Rico History: *www.elyunque.com/history.html*

Puerto Rico History: *www.centropr.org*

History of Puerto Rico: *www.solboricua.com/history.htm*

The Owlman and Others: 30th Anniversary Edition, Jonathan Downes, CFZ Press, 2006

Chapter 16: The Never-Ending Journey

Disclosure: UFO Project Launches Public Campaign: *www.share-international.org/archives/UFOs/disclosure-ufo-project.htm*

UFO Disclosure Project: *www.myspace.com/ufodisclosureproject*

Index

About the Author

Nick Redfern started his writing career in England in *Zero*, a magazine devoted to music, fashion, and the world of entertainment. He writes regularly for the British *Daily Express* newspaper, *Fate*, *Fortean Times*, and *UFO Magazine*. He is the author of nine books on a variety of mysteries, and runs the American office of the British-based Center for Fortean Zoology, the world's only full-time group dedicated to the investigation of unknown animals such as Bigfoot and the Loch Ness Monster. He has appeared on numerous television shows, including the Sci Fi Channel's *Proof Positive*, and the History Channel's *UFO Hunters*. He lives with his wife, Dana, in Dallas, Texas.

Other Books by Nick Redfern

A Covert Agenda
The FBI Files
Cosmic Crashes
Strange Secrets
Three Men Seeking Monsters
Body Snatchers in the Desert
On the Trail of the Saucer Spies
Celebrity Secrets
Man-Monkey